James Russell Lowell

Selections from the Writings of James Russell Lowell

James Russell Lowell

Selections from the Writings of James Russell Lowell

ISBN/EAN: 9783337172022

Printed in Europe, USA, Canada, Australia, Japan

Cover: Foto ©Andreas Hilbeck / pixelio.de

More available books at **www.hansebooks.com**

SELECTIONS

FROM THE WRITINGS OF

JAMES RUSSELL LOWELL—

BIRTHDAY VERSES WRITTEN IN A CHILD'S ALBUM.

THOSE awful powers on man that wait,
On man, the beggar or the king,
To hovel bare or hall of state
A magic ring that masters fate
With each succeeding birthday bring.

Therein are set four jewels rare:
Pearl winter, summer's ruby blaze,
Spring's emerald, and, than all more fair,
Fall's pensive opal, doomed to bear
A heart of fire bedreamed with haze.

To him the simple spell that knows
The spirits of the ring to sway,
Fresh power with every sunrise flows,
And royal pursuivants are those
That fly his mandates to obey.

But he that with a slackened will
Dreams of things past or things to be,
From him the charm is slipping still,
And drops, ere he suspect the ill,
Into the inexorable sea.

JANUARY 1-3

1. *Emancipation Proclamation, 1863.*

And, as the finder of some unknown realm,
Mounting a summit whence he thinks to see
On either side of him the imprisoning sea,
Beholds, above the clouds that overwhelm
The valley-land, peak after snowy peak
Stretch out of sight, each like a silver helm
Beneath its plume of smoke, sublime and bleak,
And what he thought an island finds to be
A continent to him first oped, — so we
Can from our height of Freedom look along
A boundless future, ours if we be strong.

FREEDOM.

2. *James Wolfe, 1727.*

It is no little thing, when a fresh soul
And a fresh heart, with their unmeasured scope
For good, not gravitating earthward yet,
But circling in diviner periods,
Are sent into the world.

ON THE DEATH OF A FRIEND'S CHILD.

3. *Douglas Jerrold, 1803.*

A right hand guided by an earnest soul,
With a true instinct, takes the golden prize
From out a thousand blanks.   What men call luck
Is the prerogative of valiant souls,
The fealty life pays its rightful kings.

A GLANCE BEHIND THE CURTAIN.

4. *Jakob Ludwig Grimm*, 1785.

Winter soon blows your head clear of **fog and** ~~m~~akes you see things as they are. I thank him ~~fo~~r it.   A GOOD WORD FOR WINTER.

5. *Stephen Decatur*, 1779.

As one lamp lights another, nor grows less,
So nobleness enkindleth nobleness.   YUSSOUF.

6. *Epiphany*.

An entirely new conception of the Infinite and of man's relation to it came in with Christianity. That, and not the finite, is always the background, consciously or not. It changed the scene of the last act of every drama to the next world. Endless aspiration of all the faculties became thus the ideal of Christian life, and to express it more or less perfectly the ideal of essentially Christian art.
     DANTE.

7. *Israel Putnam*, 1718.

Full many a sweet forewarning hath the mind,
    Full many a whispering of vague desire,
Ere comes the nature destined to unbind
    Its virgin zone, and all its deeps inspire, —
Low stirrings in the leaves, before the wind
    Wake all the green strings of the forest lyre,
Faint beatings in the calyx, ere the rose
Its warm voluptuous breast doth all unclose.
     A LEGEND OF BRITTANY.

8. *Robert Schumann*, 1810.

Here was genius with no volcanic explosions (the mechanic result of vulgar gunpowder often), but only as a Lapland night ; here was fame, not sought after nor worn in any cheap French fashion a ribbon at the button-hole, but so gentle, so retiring, that it seemed no more than an assured and emboldened modesty. CAMBRIDGE THIRTY YEARS AGO.

9. *Victor Emmanuel died*, 1878.

No age was e'er degenerate,
Unless men held it at too cheap a rate.
HARVARD COMMEMORATION ODE.

10. *Ethan Allen*, 1737.

All true whole men succeed ; for what is worth
Success's name, unless it be the thought,
The inward surety, to have carried out
A noble purpose to a noble end,
Although it be the gallows or the block ?
'T is only Falsehood that doth ever need
These outward shows of gain to bolster her.
A GLANCE BEHIND THE CURTAIN.

11. *Bayard Taylor*, 1825.

The Public School has done for Imagination
What shall I see in Outre-Mer, or on the way
thither, but what can be seen with eyes ? AT SEA.

12. *John Winthrop*, 1588.

! and the nobleness that li
men, sleeping, but never d
in majesty to meet thine o
t thou see it gleam in many
l pure light around thy path
a wilt nevermore be sad and

13. *S. P. Chase*, 1808.

r thinks Fact a pooty thing,
wants the banns read right ensu
t wun't noways wear the ring,
at years o' settin' up an' wooin' :
, arter all, Time's dial-plate
s cent'ries with the minute-finger,
od can't never come tu late,
gh it doos seem to try an' linger.

LATEST VIEWS OF MR. BIGLOW.

14. *Matthew F. Maury*, 1806.

ry man feels instinctively that all the
ntiments in the world weigh less than a
ly action ; and that while tenderness of
susceptibility to generous emotions are
temperament, goodness is an achieve-
will and a quality of the life.

ROUSSEAU AND THE SENTIMENTALISTS.

15. *Molière*, 1622.

ts that great hearts once brok
e cheaply in the common air ;
st we trample heedlessly
ed once in saints and heroes r
erished, opening for their race
thways to the commonplace.

16. *Duc d'Aumale*, 1822.

nd is roistering out of doors,
dows shake and my chimney
wood chimneys seem crooning
d, in their moody, minor key,
of the past the hoarse wind
in my arm-chair, and toast n

To CHARLES ELI

17. *Benjamin Franklin*, 1706.

fond in this country of what
nen (as if real success could
l this is all very well, prov
hing worth having of themse
the matter is, not where a n
re he comes out.

A GREAT PUBLIC

18. *Daniel Webster*, 1782.

ting-club where boys dispute,
le o'er their stolen fruit,
, erewhile cloister of the few,
y once flashed and Webster'
w

ose bolts of thought that all the
w ?   AN ODE FOR THE FOURTH

19. *James Watt*, 1736.

had our tea-kettle over the fire,
he cover was chattering with t
which had thus vainly begged of
d and bridled, till James Watt
o overhear it.   A MOOSEHEAD

20. *N. P. Willis*, 1807.

without reason that fame is
eath. The dust-cloud of notorie
envelopes the men who drive
ers contemporary judgment.

21. *Adolphe Monod*, 1802.

n is in itself only a farthing-c
d uncertain flame, and easily bl
ight by which the world lool

22. *Bacon*, 1561; *Byron*, 1788.

As into these vessels the water I pour,
There shall one hold less, another more,
And the water unchanged, in every case,
Shall put on the figure of the vase ;
O thou, who wouldst unity make through strife,
Canst thou fit this sign to the Water of Life ?

AMBROSE.

23. *William Page*, 1811.

We poor fools of time always hurry as if we were
he last type of man.

ITALY.

24. *Charles James Fox*, 1749.

Men prate
Of all heads to an equal grade cashiered
On level with the dullest, and expect
(Sick of no worse distemper than themselves)
A wondrous cure-all in equality ;
They reason that To-morrow must be wise
Because To-day was not, nor Yesterday,
As if good days were shapen of themselves,
Not of the very lifeblood of men's souls.

THE CATHEDRAL.

25. *Robert Burns*, 1759.

Burns, who was more out of doors than most
oets, and whose barefoot Muse got the color in her
heeks by vigorous exercise in all weathers.

A GOOD WORD FOR WINTER.

26. *Thomas Noon Talfourd*, 1795.

I have spoken of the exquisite curves of snow
surfaces. Not less rare are the tints of which they
are capable, — the faint blue of the hollows, for the
shadows in snow are always blue, and the tender
rose of higher points, as you stand with your back
to the setting sun and look upward across the soft
rondure of a hillside. I have seen within a mile of
home effects of color as lovely as any iridescence of
the Silberhorn after sundown.

A GOOD WORD FOR WINTER.

27. *W. A. Mozart*, 1756.

For, whom the heart of man shuts out,
   Sometimes the heart of God takes in,
And fences them all round about
   With silence mid the world's loud din,
And one of his great charities
   Is Music.   THE FORLORN.

28. *Charles George Gordon*, 1833.

The true ideal is not opposed to the real, nor is it
any artificial heightening thereof, but lies *in* it, and
blessed are the eyes that find it ! It is the *mens
divinior* which hides within the actual, transfiguring
matter-of-fact into matter-of-meaning for him who
has the gift of second-sight. SHAKESPEARE ONCE MORE.

29. *Swedenborg*, 1688.

His nature [Dante's] was one in which, as in Swedenborg's, a clear practical understanding was continually streamed over by the northern lights of mysticism through which the familiar stars shine with a softened and more spiritual lustre. Dante.

30. *Walter Savage Landor*, 1775.

Children learn to speak by watching the lips and catching the words of those who know how already, and poets learn in the same way from their elders. They import their raw material from any and everywhere, and the question at last comes down to this — whether an author have original force enough to assimilate all he has acquired, or that be so overmastering as to assimilate *him*. If the poet turn out the stronger, we allow him to help himself from other people with wonderful equanimity. Should a man discover the art of transmuting metals and present us with a lump of gold as large as an ostrich-egg, would it be in human nature to inquire too nicely whether he had stolen the lead ?

Chaucer.

31. *Franz Schubert*, 1797.

Feeling and music move together,
Like swan and shadow ever,   ·
Floating on a sky-blue river
In a day of cloudless weather.

To Perdita, Singing.

1. *Edmund Quincy*, 1808.

As thrills of long-hushed tone
Live in the viol, so our souls grow fine
With keen vibrations from the touch divine
Of noble natures gone.   Memoriæ Positum.

2. *Candlemas.*

Blessing she is : God made her so,
And deeds of week-day holiness
Fall from her noiseless as the snow,
Nor hath she ever chanced to know
That aught were easier than to bless.

My Love.

3. *Mendelssohn*, 1809.

One has not far to seek for book-nature, artist-nature, every variety of superinduced nature, in short, but genuine human-nature is hard to find. And how good it is ! Wholesome as a potato, fit company for any dish. The freemasonry of cultivated men is agreeable, but artificial, and I like better the natural grip with which manhood recognizes manhood.   In the Mediterranean.

4. *Josiah Quincy*, 1772.

It is such a piece of good luck to be natural ! It is the good gift which the fairy godmother brings to her prime favorites in the cradle.   Chaucer.

5. *James Otis*, 1725.

As the broad ocean endlessly unheaveth,
With the majestic beating of his heart,
The mighty tides, whereof its rightful part
Each sea-wide bay and little weed receiveth, —
So through his soul who earnestly believeth,
Life from the universal Heart doth flow,
Whereby some conquest of the eternal Woe,
By instinct of God's nature, he achieveth.

SONNET 24.

6. *Madame de Sévigné*, 1626.

Take Winter as you find him, and he turns out to
be a thoroughly honest fellow, with no nonsense in
him, and tolerating none in you, which is a great
comfort in the long run. He is not what they call
a genial critic ; but bring a real man along with
you, and you will find there is a crabbed generosity
about the old cynic that you would not exchange
for all the creamy concessions of Autumn.

A GOOD WORD FOR WINTER.

7. *Charles Dickens*, 1812.

The secret of force in writing lies not so much
in the pedigree of nouns and adjectives and verbs,
as in having something that you believe in to say,
and making the parts of speech vividly conscious
of it.

SHAKESPEARE ONCE MORE.

8. *Samuel Butler*, 1612.

No mortal ever dreams
That the scant isthmus he encamps upon
Between two oceans, one, the Stormy, passed,
And one, the Peaceful, yet to venture on,
Has been that future whereto prophets yearned
For the fulfilment of Earth's cheated hope,
Shall be that past which nerveless poets moan
As the lost opportunity of song.   THE CATHEDRAL.

9. *James Parton*, 1822.

We 're curus critters : Now ain't jes' the minute
That ever fits us easy while we 're in it ;
Long ez 't wuz futur', 't would be perfect bliss, —
Soon ez it 's past, *thet* time 's wuth ten o' this.
SUNTHIN' IN THE PASTORAL LINE.

10. *Charles Lamb*, 1775.

Fastidiousness is only another form of egotism ;
and all men who know not where to look for truth
save in the narrow well of self will find their own
image at the bottom, and mistake it for what they
are seeking.   ROUSSEAU AND THE SENTIMENTALISTS.

11. *Lydia Maria Child*, 1802.

Those love truth best who to themselves are true,
And what they dare to dream of, dare to do.
HARVARD COMMEMORATION ODE.

12. *Abraham Lincoln*, 1809.

Mr. Lincoln's faith in God was qualified by a very well-founded distrust of the wisdom of man. Perhaps it was his want of self-confidence that more than anything else won him the unlimited confidence of the people, for they felt that there would be no need of retreat from any position he had deliberately taken.

History will rank Mr. Lincoln among the most prudent of statesmen and the most successful of rulers. ABRAHAM LINCOLN.

13. *Talleyrand*, 1754.

Looking within myself, I note how thin
A plank of station, chance or prosperous fate,
Doth fence me from the clutching waves of sin.
SI DESCENDERO IN INFERNUM, ADES.

14. *Edmond About*, 1828.

Heaven is not mounted to on wings of dreams,
Nor doth the unthankful happiness of youth
Aim thitherward, but floats from bloom to bloom,
With earth's warm patch of sunshine well content.
ON THE DEATH OF A FRIEND'S CHILD.

15. *Ash Wednesday.*

'T is sorrow builds the shining ladder up,
Whose golden rounds are our calamities,
Whereon our firm feet planting, nearer God
The spirit climbs, and hath its eyes unsealed.
ON THE DEATH OF A FRIEND'S CHILD.

16. *Philip Melanchthon*, 1497.

Endurance is the crowning quality,
And patience all the passion of great hearts.

COLUMBUS.

If we could only carry that slow, imperturbable old clock of Opportunity, that never strikes a second too soon or too late, in our fobs, and push the hands forward as we can those of our watches !

CAMBRIDGE THIRTY YEARS AGO.

17. *Michael Angelo died*, 1564.

Good luck is the willing handmaid of upright, energetic character, and conscientious observance of duty.

WORDSWORTH.

18. *George Peabody*, 1795.

There has been no period of time in which wealth has been more sensible of its duties than now. It builds hospitals, it establishes missions among the poor, it endows schools. It is one of the advantages of accumulated wealth, and of the leisure it renders possible, that people have time to think of the wants and sorrows of their fellows. But all these remedies are partial and palliative merely. It is as if we should apply plasters to a single pustule of the small-pox with a view of driving out the disease. The true way is to discover and to extirpate the germs.

DEMOCRACY.

19. *First Sunday in Lent.*

Through aisles of long-drawn centuries
　My spirit walks in thought,
And to that symbol lifts its eyes
　Which God's own pity wrought ;
From Calvary shines the altar's gleam,
　The Church's East is there,
The Ages one great minster seem,
　That throbs with praise and prayer.

And all the way from Calvary down
　The carven pavement shows
Their graves who won the martyr's crown
　And safe in God repose ;
The saints of many a warring creed
　Who now in heaven have learned
That all paths to the father lead
　Where Self the feet have spurned.

GODMINSTER CHIMES.

20. *David Garrick*, 1716.

One learns more metaphysics from a single temptation than from all the philosophers.

A MOOSEHEAD JOURNAL.

21. *John Henry Newman*, 1801.

One thorn of experience is worth a whole wilderness of warning.

SHAKESPEARE ONCE MORE.

22. *George Washington*, 1732; *J. R. Lowell*, 1819.

Virginia gave us this imperial man
Cast in the massive mould
Of those high-statured ages old
Which into grander forms our mortal metal ran ;
She gave us this unblemished gentleman.

UNDER THE OLD ELM.

If God made poets for anything, it was to keep alive the traditions of the pure, the holy, and the beautiful. POPE.

23. *G. F. Händel*, 1685.

Vanity eludes recognition by its victims in more shapes, and more pleasing, than any other passion.

ROUSSEAU AND THE SENTIMENTALISTS.

24. *George William Curtis*, 1824.

It is singular how impatient men are with over-praise of others, how patient with overpraise of themselves ; and yet the one does them no injury, while the other may be their ruin.

LITERARY REMAINS OF THE REV. HOMER WILBUR.

25. *Charles C. Pinckney*, 1766.

Mishaps are like knives, that either serve us or cut us, as we grasp them by the blade or the handle.

CAMBRIDGE THIRTY YEARS AGO.

FEBRUARY 26-29

26. *Second Sunday in Lent.*

There are three short and simple words, the hardest of all to pronounce in any language (and I suspect they were no easier before the confusion of tongues), but which no man or nation that cannot utter can claim to have arrived at manhood. Those words are, *I was wrong.* LETTER OF THE REV. HOMER WILBUR.

27. *Henry Wadsworth Longfellow*, 1807.

With loving breath of all the winds his name
Is blown about the world, but to his friends
A sweeter secret hides behind his fame,
And love steals shyly through the loud acclaim,
To murmur a *God bless you !* and there ends.
To H. W. L.

28. *Michel de Montaigne*, 1533.

For manhood is the one immortal thing
Beneath Time's changeful sky,
And, where it lightened once, from age to age,
Men come to learn, in grateful pilgrimage,
That length of days is knowing when to die.
ODE READ AT CONCORD.

29. *Rossini*, 1792.

They think I burrow from the sun,
In darkness, all alone, and weak ;
Such loss were gain if He were won,
For 't is the sun's own Sun I seek.
THE MINER.

1. *W. D. Howells*, 1837.

Talent is that which is in a man's power ; genius is that in whose power a man is.

ROUSSEAU AND THE SENTIMENTALISTS.

2. *Sir Thomas Bodley*, 1544.

These rugged, wintry days I scarce could bear,
Did I not know, that, in the early spring,
When wild March winds upon their errands sing,
Thou wouldst return, bursting on the still air,
Like those same winds, when, startled from their
      lair,
They hunt up violets, and free swift brooks
From icy cares, even as thy clear looks
Bid my heart bloom, and sing, and break all care :
When drops with welcome rain the April day,
My flowers shall find their April in thine eyes,
Save there the rain in dreamy clouds doth stay,
As loath to fall out of those happy skies ;
Yet sure, my love, thou art most like to May,
That comes with steady sun when April dies.

IN ABSENCE.

3. *Edmund Waller*, 1606.

He is a coward, who would borrow
A charm against the present sorrow
From the vague Future's promise of delight.

TO THE FUTURE.

4. *Third Sunday in Lent.*

The divine reason must forever manifest itself anew in the lives of men, and that as individuals. This atonement with God, this identification of the man with the truth, so that right action shall not result from the lower reason of utility, but from the higher of a will so purified of self as to sympathize by instinct with the eternal laws, is not something that can be done once for all, that can become historic and traditional, a dead flower pressed between the leaves of the family Bible, but must be renewed in every generation, and in the soul of every man, that it may be valid.   DANTE.

5. *James Madison,* 1751.

Three roots bear up Dominion : Knowledge, Will, —
These twain are strong, but stronger yet the
     third, —
Obedience, — 't is the great tap-root that still,
Knit round the rock of Duty, is not stirred,
Though Heaven-loosed tempests spend their utmost
     skill.   THE WASHERS OF THE SHROUD.

6. *Michael Angelo,* 1475.

Michael Angelo created a new world in which everything was colossal.

     A FEW BITS OF ROMAN MOSAIC.

7. *Sir Edwin Landseer*, 1802.

Browning has given the best picture of St. Peter's on a festival day, sketching it with a few verses in his large style. And doubtless it is the scene of the grandest spectacles which the world can see in these latter days.　　　A FEW BITS OF ROMAN MOSAIC.

8. *Christopher P. Cranch*, 1813.

Where'er a human heart doth wear
　Joy's myrtle-wreath or sorrow's gyves,
　Where'er a human spirit strives
After a life more true and fair,
There is the true man's birthplace grand,
His is a world-wide fatherland !

THE FATHERLAND.

9. *William Cobbett*, 1762.

As soon as we have discovered the word for our joy or sorrow we are no longer its serfs, but its lords.　　　KEATS.

10. *Alexander III. of Russia*, 1845.

When I wuz younger 'n wut you see me now, —
Nothin' from Adam's fall to Huldy's bonnet,
Thet I warn 't full-cocked with my jedgment on it ;
But now I 'm gittin' on in life, I find
It 's a sight harder to make up my mind.

SUNTHIN' IN THE PASTORAL LINE.

11. *Fourth Sunday in Lent.*

God is not dumb, that He should speak no more ;
If thou hast wanderings in the wilderness
And find'st not Sinai, 't is thy soul is poor ;
There towers the mountain of the Voice no less,
Which whoso seeks shall find.   BIBLIOLATRES.

12. *Bishop Berkeley,* 1684.

Peace is more strong than war, and gentleness,
  Where force were vain, makes conquest o'er the
    wave ;
And love lives on and hath a power to bless,
  When they who loved are hidden in the grave.
      ELEGY ON THE DEATH OF DR. CHANNING.

13. *Joseph Priestley,* 1733.

Count me o'er earth's chosen heroes, — they were
  souls that stood alone,
While the men they agonized for hurled the con-
  tumelious stone,
Stood serene, and down the future saw the golden
  beam incline
To the side of perfect justice, mastered by their
  faith divine,
By one man's plain truth to manhood and to God's
  supreme design.   THE PRESENT CRISIS.

14. *Victor Emmanuel*, 1820 ; *Humbert*, 1844.

The brave makes danger opportunity ;
The waverer, paltering with the chance sublime,
Dwarfs it to peril. THE WASHERS OF THE SHROUD.

15. *Andrew Jackson*, 1767.

No very large share of truth falls to the apprehension of any one man ; let him keep it sacred and beware of repeating it till it turn to falsehood on his lips by becoming ritual. CARLYLE.

16. *Caroline Herschel*, 1750.

Truth is eternal, but her effluence,
With endless change is fitted to the hour.
A GLANCE BEHIND THE CURTAIN.

17. *Madame Roland*, 1754.

I cannot conceive the confusion of tongues to have been the curse of Babel, since I esteem my ignorance of other languages as a kind of Martello-tower, in which I am safe from the furious bombardments of foreign garrulity.
LETTER OF THE REV. HOMER WILBUR.

Indeed, the power to express the same nothing in ten different languages is something to be dreaded rather than admired. It gives a horrible advantage to dulness. LIFE AND LETTERS OF JAMES GATES PERCIVAL.

18. *Fifth Sunday in Lent.*

All God's angels come to us disguised ;
Sorrow and sickness, poverty and death,
One after other lift their frowning masks,
And we behold the seraph's face beneath,
All radiant with the glory and the calm
Of having looked upon the front of God.
With every anguish of our earthly part
The spirit's sight grows clearer.

ON THE DEATH OF A FRIEND'S CHILD.

19. *David Livingstone,* 1813.

People are apt to confound mere alertness of mind with attention. The one is but the flying abroad of all the faculties to the open doors and windows at every passing rumor ; the other is the concentration of every one of them in a single focus, as in the alchemist over his alembic at the moment of expected projection. Attention is the stuff that memory is made of, and memory is accumulated genius.

LITERARY REMAINS OF THE REV. HOMER WILBUR.

20. *Sir Isaac Newton died,* 1727.

How very small a part of the world we truly live in is represented by what speaks to us through the senses when compared with that vast realm of the mind which is peopled by memory and imagination, and with such shining inhabitants !

BOOKS AND LIBRARIES.

21. *Sebastian Bach*, 1685.

It [the sea] reminds me of organ music and my good friend Sebastian Bach. A fugue or two will do very well ; but a concert made up of nothing else is altogether too epic for me. AT SEA.

22. *Emperor William of Germany*, 1797.

Nor can I count him happiest who has never
Been forced with his own hand his chains to sever,
And for himself find out the way divine ;
He never knew the aspirer's glorious pains,
He never earned the struggle's priceless gains.
TRIAL.

23. *Laplace*, 1749.

There is something solid and doughty in the man that can rise from defeat, the stuff of which victories are made in due time, when we are able to choose our position better, and the sun is at our back. DRYDEN.

24. *Longfellow died*, 1882.

Surely if skill in song the shears may stay
And of its purpose cheat the charmed abyss,
If our poor life be lengthened by a lay,
He shall not go, although his presence may,
And the next age in praise shall double this.
To H. W. L.

25. *Palm Sunday.*

There are who triumph in a losing cause,
Who can put on defeat, as 't were a wreath
Unwithering in the adverse popular breath,
　　Safe from the blasting demagogue's applause ;
　　'T is they who stand for Freedom and God's
　　　　laws. 　　　　To John G. Palfrey.

26. *Nathaniel Bowditch,* 1773.

A race of nobles may die out,
A royal line may leave no heir ;
Wise Nature sets no guards about
Her pewter plate and wooden ware.
But they fail not, the kinglier breed,
Who starry diadems attain ;
To dungeon, axe, and stake succeed
Heirs of the old heroic strain. 　　Kossuth.

27. *Vera Cruz taken by Scott,* 1847.

To have stored moral capital enough to meet the
drafts of Death at sight, must be an unmatched
tonic. 　　　　A Great Public Character.

28. *Thomas Clarkson,* 1760.

Death ever fronts the wise ;
Not fearfully, but with clear promises
Of larger life. 　　　　Prometheus.

29. *Swedenborg died*, 1772.

Then to side with Truth is noble when we share her
    wretched crust,
Ere her cause bring fame and profit, and 't is pros-
    perous to be just ;
Then it is the brave man chooses, while the coward
    stands aside,
Doubting in his abject spirit, till his Lord is cruci-
    fied.   The Present Crisis.

30. *Good Friday.*

By the light of burning heretics Christ's bleeding
    feet I track,
Toiling up new Calvaries ever with the cross that
    turns not back,
And these mounts of anguish number how each gen-
    eration learned
One new word of that grand *Credo* which in prophet-
    hearts hath burned
Since the first man stood God-conquered, with his
    face to heaven upturned.   The Present Crisis.

31. *Joseph Haydn*, 1732.

Hide still, best Good, in subtile wise,
    Beyond my nature's utmost scope ;
Be ever absent from mine eyes
    To be twice present in my hope !   The Miner.

1. *Easter Day.*

O chime of sweet Saint Charity,
 Peal soon that Easter morn
When Christ for all shall risen be,
 And in all hearts new-born !

GODMINSTER CHIMES.

2. *H. C. Andersen,* 1805.

Those Easter pomps, where the antique world marches visibly before you in gilded mail and crimson doublet, refresh the eyes, and are good so long as they continue to be merely spectacle. But if one thinks for a moment of the servant of the servants of the Lord in cloth of gold, borne on men's shoulders, or of the children receiving the blessing of their Holy Father, with a regiment of French soldiers to protect the father from the children, it becomes a little sad.

A FEW BITS OF ROMAN MOSAIC.

3. *Washington Irving,* 1783.

What ! Irving ? thrice welcome,
Warm heart and fine brain,
You bring back the happiest spirit from Spain,
And the gravest sweet humor, that ever were there
Since Cervantes met death in his gentle despair.

A FABLE FOR CRITICS.

4. *Benjamin Peirce*, 1809.

Few men learn the highest use of books. After lifelong study many a man discovers too late that to have had the philosopher's stone availed nothing without the philosopher to use it.

BOOKS AND LIBRARIES.

5. *Sir Henry Havelock*, 1795.

Men's monuments, grown old, forget their names
They should eternize, but the place
Where shining souls have passed imbibes a grace
Beyond mere earth ; some sweetness of their fames
Leaves in the soil its unextinguished trace,
Pungent, pathetic, sad with nobler aims,
That penetrates our lives and heightens them or
    shames.   UNDER THE OLD ELM.

6. *Raphael born*, 1483, *and died*, 1520.

One beauty, at its highest, prophesies
That by whose side it shall seem mean and poor.

SONNET 17.

7. *Wordsworth*, 1770.

If it be one of the baser consolations, it is also one of the most disheartening concomitants of long life, that we get used to everything. Two things, perhaps, retain their freshness more perdurably than the rest, — the return of spring, and the more poignant utterances of the poets. And here, I think, Wordsworth holds his own with the best.

ADDRESS AS PRESIDENT OF THE WORDSWORTH SOCIETY.

8. *G. W. Greene*, 1811.

Wealth and rule slip down with Fortune, as her
  wheel turns round ;
He who keeps his faith, he only cannot be dis-
  crowned. MAHMOOD THE IMAGE BREAKER.

9. *Fisher Ames*, 1758.

The world always judges a man (and rightly
enough, too) by his little faults, which he shows a
hundred times a day, rather than by his great vir-
tues, which he discloses perhaps but once in a lifetime, and to a single person, — nay, in proportion
as they are rarer, and he is nobler, is shyer of let-
ting their existence be known at all.
  CAMBRIDGE THIRTY YEARS AGO.

10. *Lew Wallace*, 1827.

Nor deem that acts heroic wait on chance
Or easy were as in a boy's romance ;
The man's whole life preludes the single deed
That shall decide if his inheritance
Be with the sifted few of matchless breed,
Our race's sap and sustenance,
Or with the unmotived herd that only sleep and
  feed. UNDER THE OLD ELM.

11. *Edward Everett*, 1794.

But Chance is like an amberill, — it don't take twice
  to lose it.
  BIRDOFREDUM SAWIN, ESQ., TO MR. HOSEA BIGLOW.

12. *Henry Clay, 1777.*

The busy world shoves angrily aside
The man who stands with arms akimbo set,
Until occasion tells him what to do ;
And he who waits to have his task marked out
Shall die and leave his errand unfulfilled.

A GLANCE BEHIND THE CURTAIN.

13. *Fall of Fort Sumter, 1861.*

Bow down, dear Land, for thou hast found release !
Thy God, in these distempered days,
Hath taught thee the sure wisdom of His ways,
And through thine enemies hath wrought thy peace !
Bow down in prayer and praise !
No poorest in thy borders but may now
Lift to the juster skies a man's enfranchised brow.

HARVARD COMMEMORATION ODE.

14. *Lincoln assassinated, 1865.*

But democracies have likewise their finer instincts. I have also seen the wisest statesman and most pregnant speaker of our generation, a man of humble birth and ungainly manners, of little culture beyond what his own genius supplied, become more absolute in power than any monarch of modern times through the reverence of his countrymen for his honesty, his wisdom, his sincerity, his faith in God and man, and the nobly humane simplicity of his character. . . . Institutions which could bear and breed such men as Lincoln and Emerson had surely some energy for good.

DEMOCRACY.

15. *John Lothrop Motley*, 1814.

Amid all the fruitless turmoil and miscarriage of the world, if there be one thing steadfast and of favorable omen, one thing to make optimism distrust its own obscure distrust, it is the rooted instinct in men to admire what is better and more beautiful than themselves. DEMOCRACY.

16. *Battle of Culloden*, 1746.

Aprul's come back; the swellin' buds of oak
Dim the fur hillsides with a purplish smoke;
The brooks are loose an', singing to be seen,
(Like gals,) make all the hollers soft an' green;
The birds are here, for all the season's late;
They take the sun's height an' don' never wait;
Soon 'z he officially declares it's spring
Their light hearts lift 'em on a north'ard wing,
An' th' ain't an acre, fur ez you can hear,
Can't by the music tell the time o' year.
MR. HOSEA BIGLOW'S SPEECH IN MARCH MEETING.

17. *William Gilmore Simms*, 1806.

I think the human mind pines more or less where everything is new, and is better for a diet of stale bread. A MOOSEHEAD JOURNAL.

18. *Luther before the Diet of Worms*, 1521.

Get but the truth once uttered, and 't is like
A star new-born, that drops into its place.
A GLANCE BEHIND THE CURTAIN.

19. *Lexington and Concord*, 1775.

It was the drums of Naseby and Dunbar that gathered the minute-men on Lexington Common ; it was the red dint of the axe on Charles's block that marked One in our era.

NEW ENGLAND TWO CENTURIES AGO.

20. *W. H. Furness*, 1802.

He reads most wisely who thinks everything into a book that it is capable of holding, and it is the stamp and token of a great book so to incorporate itself with our own being, so to quicken our insight and stimulate our thought, as to make us feel as if we helped to create it while we read.

BOOKS AND LIBRARIES.

21. *Charlotte Brontë*, 1816.

Whither leads the path
To ampler fates that leads ?
Not down through flowery meads,
   To reap an aftermath
    Of youth's vainglorious weeds,
    But up the steep, amid the wrath
   And shock of deadly-hostile creeds,
   Where the world's best hope and stay
By battle's flashes gropes a desperate way,
And every turf the fierce foot clings to bleeds.

HARVARD COMMEMORATION ODE.

22. *Henry Fielding,* 1707.

Enthusiasm begets enthusiasm, eloquence produces conviction for the moment, but it is only by truth to nature and the everlasting intuitions of mankind that those abiding influences are won that enlarge from generation to generation.

ROUSSEAU AND THE SENTIMENTALISTS.

23. *Shakespeare born,* 1564, *and died,* 1616.

And it is certainly true that the material of thought reacts upon the thought itself. Shakespeare himself would have been commonplace had he been paddocked in a thinly-shaven vocabulary, and Phidias, had he worked in wax, only a more inspired Mrs. Jarley. A man is known, says the proverb, by the company he keeps, and not only so, but made by it.

BOOKS AND LIBRARIES.

24. *Anthony Trollope,* 1815.

But higher even than the genius we rate the character of this unique man, and the grand impersonality of what he wrote. What has he told us of himself ? In our self-exploiting nineteenth century, with its melancholy liver-complaint, how serene and high he seems ! If he had sorrows, he has made them the woof of everlasting consolation to his kind ; and if, as poets are wont to whine, the outward world was cold to him, its biting air did but trace itself in loveliest frost-work of fancy on the many windows of that self-centred and cheerful soul.

SHAKESPEARE ONCE MORE.

25. *Oliver Cromwell*, 1599.

One may find grandeur in a starlight night without caring to ask what it means, save grandeur and consolation. . . . One may think roses as good in their way as cabbages, though the latter would make a better show in the witness-box if cross-examined as to their usefulness. EMERSON THE LECTURER.

26. *J. L. Uhland*, 1787.

Spring is a fickle mistress, who either does not know her own mind, or is so long in making it up, whether you shall have her or not have her, that one gets tired at last of her pretty miffs and reconciliations. You go to her to be cheered up a bit, and ten to one catch her in the sulks, expecting you to find enough good humor for both.

A GOOD WORD FOR WINTER.

27. *U. S. Grant*, 1822.

To front a lie in arms and not to yield,
This shows, methinks, God's plan
And measure of a stalwart man.

COMMEMORATION ODE.

28. *James Monroe*, 1758.

An' his gret sword behind him sloped away
Long 'z a man's speech thet dunno wut to say.

SUNTHIN' IN THE PASTORAL LINE.

29. *Oliver Ellsworth*, 1745.

Leave what to do and what to spare
To the inspiring moment's care,
  Nor ask for payment
Of fame or gold, but just to wear
  Unspotted raiment.   Fancy's Casuistry.

30. *Duke of Argyll*, 1823.

It is as easy — and no easier — to be natural in
a *salon* as in a swamp, if one do not aim at it, for
what we call unnaturalness always has its spring in
a man's thinking too much about himself.
    Thoreau.

MAY

1. *Joseph Addison*, 1672.

Jes' so with poets : Wut they 've airly read,
Git kind o' worked into their heart an' head,

.   .   .   .

This makes 'em think our fust of May is May,
Which 't ain't, for all the almanicks can say.
    Sunthin' in the Pastoral Line.

2. *John Gorham Palfrey*, 1796.

I take my May down from the happy shelf
Where perch the world's rare song-birds in a row.
    Under the Willows.

3. *Macchiavelli*, 1469.

There is no good in arguing with the inevitable. The only argument available with an east wind is to put on your overcoat. DEMOCRACY.

4. *William H. Prescott*, 1796.

In spite of the proverb, great effects do not follow from small causes, — that is, disproportionately small, — but from adequate causes acting under certain required conditions. To contrast the size of the oak with that of the parent acorn, as if the poor seed had paid all costs from its slender strong-box, may serve for a child's wonder ; but the real miracle lies in that divine league which bound all the forces of nature to the service of the tiny germ in fulfilling its destiny. ABRAHAM LINCOLN.

5. *Empress Eugénie*, 1826.

Year by year, more and more of the world gets disenchanted. Even the icy privacy of the arctic and antarctic circles is invaded. Our youth are no longer ingenious, as indeed no ingenuity is demanded of them. Everything is accounted for, everything cut and dried, and the world may be put together as easily as the fragments of a dissected map. The Mysterious bounds nothing now on the North, South, East, or West. We have played Jack Horner with our earth, till there is never a plum left in it. AT SEA.

6. *Lord Frederick Cavendish and Mr. Burke assassinated,*
1882.

Beauty and Truth, and all that these contain,
Drop not like ripened fruit about our feet ;
   We climb to them through years of sweat and
      pain ;
   Without long struggle, none did e'er attain
The downward look from Quiet's blissful seat :
   Though present loss may be the hero's part,
   Yet none can rob him of the victor heart
Whereby the broad-realmed future is subdued.

To John G. Palfrey.

7. *Robert Browning,* 1812.

Browning, by far the richest nature of the time,
becomes more difficult, draws nearer to the all-for-
point fashion of the *concettisti* with every poem he
writes.   Swinburne's Tragedies.

8. *Alessandro Manzoni,* 1785.

History is, indeed, mainly the biography of a few
imperial men, and forces home upon us the useful
lesson how infinitesimally important our own private
affairs are to the universe in general. History is
clarified experience, and yet how little do men profit
by it ; nay, how should we expect it of those who so
seldom are taught anything by their own !

Books and Libraries.

9. *Sismondi*, 1773.

Desultory reading, except as conscious pastime, hebetates the brain and slackens the bow-string of Will. It communicates as little intelligence as the messages that run along the telegraph wire to the birds that perch on it.   BOOKS AND LIBRARIES.

10. *Ascension Day.*

A higher mode of belief is the best exorciser, because it makes the spiritual at one with the actual world instead of hostile, or at best alien. It has been the grossly material interpretations of spiritual doctrine that have given occasion to the two extremes of superstition and unbelief.   WITCHCRAFT.

11. *Dr. John Brown died*, 1882.

Though I own up I like our back'ard springs
Thet kind o' haggle with their greens an' things,
An' when you 'most give up, 'ithout more words
Toss the fields full o' blossoms, leaves, an' birds :
Thet 's Northun natur', slow an' apt to doubt,
But when it *doos* git stirred, ther' 's no gin-out !
    SUNTHIN' IN THE PASTORAL LINE.

12. *Dante Gabriel Rossetti*, 1828.

It is our lawless and uncertain thoughts, it is the indefiniteness of our impressions, that fill darkness, whether mental or physical, with spectres and hobgoblins.   DEMOCRACY.

13. *Empress Maria Theresa*, 1717.

I grieve not that ripe Knowledge takes away
The charm that Nature to my childhood wore,
For, with that insight, cometh, day by day,
A greater bliss than wonder was before ;
The real doth not clip the poet's wings, —
To win the secret of a weed's plain heart
Reveals some clew to spiritual things,
And stumbling guess becomes firm-footed art.

SONNET 25.

14. *Constitutional Convention met*, 1787.

Perhaps it is fortunate to have an unwritten Constitution, for men are prone to be tinkering the work of their own hands, whereas they are more willing to let time and circumstance mend or modify what time and circumstance have made.　　DEMOCRACY.

15. *Prince Metternich*, 1773.

Thou art my tropics and mine Italy ;
To look at thee unlocks a warmer clime ;
　　The eyes thou givest me
Are in the heart and heed not space or time.

TO A DANDELION.

16. *William H. Seward*, 1801.

Every truth of morals must be redemonstrated in the experience of the individual man before he is capable of utilizing it.　　DANTE.

17. *Edward Jenner*, 1749.

Wrong ever builds on quicksands, but the Right
To the firm centre lays its moveless base.
The tyrant trembles, if the air but stirs
The innocent ringlets of a child's free hair,
And crouches, when the thought of some great spirit,
With world-wide murmur, like a rising gale,
Over men's hearts, as over standing corn,
Rushes, and bends them to its own strong will.

PROMETHEUS.

18. *Samuel Hoar*, 1778.

Alas, it is we ourselves that are getting buried
alive under this avalanche of earthy impertinences!
It is we who, while we might each in his humble
way be helping our fellows into the right path, or
adding one block to the climbing spire of a fine soul,
are willing to become mere sponges saturated from
the stagnant goosepond of village gossip. This is
the kind of news we compass the globe to catch,
fresh from Bungtown Centre, when we might have
it fresh from heaven by the electric lines of poet or
prophet.

BOOKS AND LIBRARIES.

19. *Hawthorne died*, 1864.

The Puritanism of the past found its unwilling
poet in Hawthorne, the rarest creative imagination
of the century. The rarest in some ideal respects
since Shakespeare.

THOREAU.

20. *Whitsunday.*

We see but half the causes of our deeds,
Seeking them wholly in the outer life,
And heedless of the encircling spirit-world,
Which, though unseen, is felt, and sows in us
All germs of pure and world-wide purposes.
From one stage of our being to the next
We pass unconscious o'er a slender bridge,
The momentary work of unseen hands,
Which crumbles down behind us ; looking back,
We see the other shore, the gulf between,
And, marvelling how we won to where we stand,
Content ourselves to call the builder Chance.

A GLANCE BEHIND THE CURTAIN.

21. *Elizabeth Fry,* 1780.

Not suffering, but faint heart, is worst of woes.

THE WASHERS OF THE SHROUD.

22. *Richard Wagner,* 1813.

The Opera is the closest approach we have to the
ancient drama in the essentials of structure and
presentation ; and could we have a *libretto* founded
on a national legend and written by one man of
genius to be filled out and accompanied by the music
of another, we might hope for something of the
same effect upon the stage.   SWINBURNE'S TRAGEDIES.

23. *Thomas Hood,* 1798.

The only conclusive evidence of a man's sincerity is that he give *himself* for a principle. Words, money, all things else, are comparatively easy to give away ; but when a man makes a gift of his daily life and practice, it is plain that the truth, whatever it may be, has taken possession of him.

ROUSSEAU AND THE SENTIMENTALISTS.

24. *Queen Victoria,* 1819.

Under a wise, cultivated, and firm-handed monarch also, the national feeling of England grew rapidly more homogeneous and intense, the rather as the womanhood of the sovereign stimulated a more chivalric loyalty, — while the new religion, of which she was the defender, helped to make England morally, as it was geographically, insular to the continent of Europe.

SHAKESPEARE ONCE MORE.

25. *R. W. Emerson,* 1803.

Search for his eloquence in his books and you will perchance miss it, but meanwhile you will find that it has kindled all your thoughts.

EMERSON THE LECTURER.

26. *Joseph S. Buckminster,* 1784.

Without earnest convictions, no great or sound literature is conceivable.

DRYDEN.

27. *Dante*, 1265.

The secret of Dante's power is not far to seek. Whoever can express *himself* with the full force of unconscious sincerity will be found to have uttered something ideal and universal.   DANTE.

In what I think to be the sublimest reach to which poetry has risen, the conclusion of the "Paradiso," Dante tell us that within the three whirling rings of vari-colored light that symbolize the wisdom, the power, and the love of God, he seems to see the image of man.

ADDRESS AS PRESIDENT OF THE WORDSWORTH SOCIETY.

28. *Louis Agassiz*, 1807.

His magic was not far to seek, —
He was so human ! whether strong or weak,
Far from his kind he neither sank nor soared,
But sate an equal guest at every board :
No beggar ever felt him condescend,
Nor prince presume ; for still himself he bare
At manhood's simple level, and where'er
He met a stranger, there he left a friend.

AGASSIZ.

29. *Patrick Henry*, 1736.

All great poets have their message to deliver us from something higher than they.   DANTE.

30. *Decoration Day.*

Many loved Truth, and lavished life's best oil
  Amid the dust of books to find her,
Content at last, for guerdon of their toil,
  With the cast mantle she hath left behind her.
    Many in sad faith sought for her,
    Many with crossed hands sighed for her ;
    But these, our brothers, fought for her,
    At life's dear peril wrought for her,
    So loved her that they died for her.
HARVARD COMMEMORATION ODE.

31. *John A. Andrew*, 1818.

      What a day
To sun me and do nothing ! Nay, I think
Merely to bask and ripen is sometimes
The student's wiser business.
UNDER THE WILLOWS.

JUNE

1. *Prince Imperial killed*, 1879.

Away, unfruitful love of books,
For whose vain idiom we reject
The soul's more native dialect.   AL FRESCO.

2. *John G. Saxe*, 1816.

For remember that there is nothing less profitable than scholarship for the mere sake of scholarship, nor anything more wearisome in the attainment.
BOOKS AND LIBRARIES.

3. *Sydney Smith,* 1771.

Heaven's cup held down to me I drain,
The sunshine mounts and spurs my brain ;
Bathing in grass, with thirsty eye
I suck the last drop of the sky ;
With each hot sense I draw to the lees
The quickening out-door influences,
And empty to each radiant comer
A supernaculum of summer.   Eurydice.

4. *Lord Wolseley,* 1833.

June's bridesman, poet o' the year,
Gladness on wings, the bobolink, is here ;
Half-hid in tip-top apple-blooms he swings,
Or climbs aginst the breeze with quiverin' wings,
Or, givin' way to 't in a mock despair,
Runs down, a brook o' laughter, thru the air.
                  Sunthin' in the Pastoral Line.

5. *Counts Egmont and Horn beheaded,* 1568.

There is something inexpressibly dear to me in
these old friendships of a lifetime. . . . I love to
bring these aborigines back to the mansuetude they
showed to the early voyagers, and before (forgive
the involuntary pun) they had grown accustomed
to man and knew his savage ways. And they re-
pay your kindness with a sweet familiarity too deli-
cate ever to breed contempt.
                  My Garden Acquaintance.

6. *Corneille*, 1606.

Nor th' airth don't git put out with me,
   Thet love her 'z though she wuz a woman ;
Why, th' a'n't a bird upon the tree
   But half forgives my bein' human.

MR. HOSEA BIGLOW TO THE EDITOR.

7. *The Field of the Cloth of Gold*, 1520.

The crows flapped over by twos and threes,
In the pool drowsed the cattle up to their knees,
   The little birds sang as if it were
   The one day of summer in all the year,
And the very leaves seemed to sing on the trees.

THE VISION OF SIR LAUNFAL.

8. *Charles Reade*, 1814.

Summer on field and hill, in heart and brain,
All life washed clean in this high tide of June.

UNDER THE WILLOWS.

9. *Charles Dickens died*, 1870.

What is the reason that all children are geniuses,
(though they contrive so soon to outgrow that dangerous quality,) except that they never cross-examine themselves on the subject ? The moment that process begins, their speech loses its gift of unexpectedness, and they become as tediously impertinent as the rest of us.

ROUSSEAU AND THE SENTIMENTALISTS.

10. *Francis L. Hawks*, 1798.

Not only around our infancy
Doth heaven with all its splendors lie ;
Daily, with souls that cringe and plot,
We Sinais climb and know it not.

THE VISION OF SIR LAUNFAL.

11. *Ben Jonson*, 1574.

Hushed with broad sunlight lies the hill,
And, minuting the long day's loss,
The cedar's shadow, slow and still,
Creeps o'er its dial of gray moss.

Warm noon brims full the valley's cup,
The aspen's leaves are scarce astir ;
Only the little mill sends up
Its busy, never-ceasing burr.

BEAVER BROOK.

12. *Charles Kingsley*, 1819.

O Faith ! if thou art strong, thine opposite
Is mighty also, and the dull fool's sneer
Hath ofttimes shot chill palsy through the arm
Just lifted to achieve its crowning deed.

COLUMBUS.

13. *Thomas Arnold*, 1795.

Children are God's apostles, day by day
Sent forth to preach of love, and hope, and peace.

ON THE DEATH OF A FRIEND'S CHILD.

14. *Harriet Beecher Stowe,* 1811.

Yes, a great heart is hers, one that dares to go in
To the prison, the slave-hut, the alleys of sin,
And to bring into each, or to find there some line,
Of the never completely out-trampled divine.

A FABLE FOR CRITICS.

15. *Magna Charta signed,* 1215.

The world of the imagination is not the world of
abstraction and nonentity, as some conceive, but a
world formed out of chaos by a sense of the beauty
that is in man and the earth on which he dwells.
It is the realm of Might-be, our haven of refuge
from the shortcomings and disillusions of life. . . .
Do we believe, then, that God gave us in mockery
this splendid faculty of sympathy with things that
are a joy forever? For my part, I believe that
the love and study of works of imagination is of
practical utility in a country so profoundly material
(or, as we like to call it, practical) in its leading
tendencies as ours. BOOKS AND LIBRARIES.

16. *Judah Touro,* 1775.

Who speaks the truth stabs Falsehood to the heart,
And his mere word makes despots tremble more
Than ever Brutus with his dagger could. L'ENVOI.

17. *Bunker Hill*, 1775.

Experience is a dumb, dead thing,
The victory 's in believing.   To ———.

18. *Waterloo*, 1815.

Trust me, 't is something to be cast
Face to face with one's Self at last,
To be taken out of the fuss and strife,
The endless clatter of plate and knife,
The bore of books and the bores of the street,
From the singular mess we agree to call Life,
Where that is best which the most fools vote is,
And to be set down on one's own two feet
So nigh to the great warm heart of God,
You almost seem to feel it beat.

PICTURES FROM APPLEDORE.

19. *Pascal*, 1623.

All birds during the pairing season become more
or less sentimental, and murmur soft nothings in a
tone very unlike the grinding-organ repetition and
loudness of their habitual song. The crow is very
comical as a lover, and to hear him trying to soften
his croak to the proper Saint Preux standard has
something the effect of a Mississippi boatman quot-
ing Tennyson. Yet there are few things to my ear
more melodious than his caw of a clear winter morning, as it drops to you filtered through five hundred
fathoms of crisp blue air. MY GARDEN ACQUAINTANCE.

20. *Accession of Queen Victoria, 1837.*

Frank-hearted hostess of the field and wood,
Gypsy, whose roof is every spreading tree,
June is the pearl of our New England year.
Still a surprisal, though expected long,
Her coming startles.   Long she lies in wait,
Makes many a feint, peeps forth, draws coyly back,
Then, from some southern ambush in the sky,
With one great gush of blossom storms the world.

UNDER THE WILLOWS.

21. *Earl of Dufferin, 1826.*

If poems die, it is because there was never true life in them, that is, that true poetic vitality which no depth of thought, no airiness of fancy, no sincerity of feeling, can singly communicate, but which leaps throbbing at touch of that shaping faculty, the imagination.

SPENSER.

22. *Thomas Day, 1748.*

It is not a great Xerxes army of words, but a compact Greek ten thousand, that march safely down to posterity.

WORDSWORTH.

23. *Midsummer Eve.*

Pan leaps and pipes all summer long,
   The fairies dance each full-mooned night,
Would we but doff our lenses strong,
   And trust our wiser eyes' delight.

THE FOOT-PATH.

24. *St. John Baptist.*

Too many noble souls have thought and died,
  Too many mighty poets lived and sung,
And our good Saxon, from lips purified
  With martyr fire, throughout the world hath rung
Too long to have God's holy cause denied.

SONNET VI.

25. *Lucius Manlius Sargent,* 1786.

I care not how men trace their ancestry,
  To ape or Adam ; let them please their whim ;
But I in June am midway to believe
A tree among my far progenitors,
Such sympathy is mine with all the race.

UNDER THE WILLOWS.

26. *Philip Doddridge,* 1702.

Opinions are " as handy," to borrow our Yankee proverb, " as a pocket in a shirt," and, I may add, as hard to come at.   HARVARD ANNIVERSARY ADDRESS.

27. *Sir William Pepperell,* 1696.

The greatest poets, I think, have found man more interesting than nature, have considered nature as no more than the necessary scenery, artistically harmful if too pompous or obtrusive, before which man acts his tragi-comedy of life.

ADDRESS AS PRESIDENT OF THE WORDSWORTH SOCIETY.

28. *J. J. Rousseau*, 1712.

"Do right though the heavens fall" is an admirable precept so long as the heavens do not take you at your word and come down about your ears — still worse about those of your neighbors. It is a rule rather of private than public obligation — for indeed it is the doing of right that *keeps* the heavens from falling. Don Quixote.

29. *St. Peter*.

What men call luck
Is the prerogative of valiant souls,
The fealty life pays its rightful kings.
A Glance Behind the Curtain.

30. *Leopardi*, 1798.

The robin has a bad reputation among people who do not value themselves less for being fond of cherries. There is, I admit, a spice of vulgarity in him, and his song is rather of the Bloomfield sort, too largely ballasted with prose. . . . But for a' that and twice as muckle 's a' that, I would not exchange him for all the cherries that ever came out of Asia Minor. With whatever faults, he has not wholly forfeited that superiority which belongs to the children of nature. My Garden Acquaintance.

1. *First Day of Gettysburg,* 1863.

And for associations, if one have not the wit to make them for himself out of his native earth, no ready-made ones of other men will avail him much. Lexington is none the worse to me for not being in Greece, nor Gettysburg that its name is not Marathon.   On a Certain Condescension in Foreigners.

2. *C. W. von Gluck,* 1714.

Like to a mighty heart the music seemed,
  That yearns with melodies it cannot speak,
Until, in grand despair of what it dreamed,
  In the agony of effort it doth break,
Yet triumphs breaking ; on it rushed and streamed
And wantoned in its might, as when a lake,
Long pent among the mountains, bursts its walls
And in one crowding gush leaps forth and falls.
                              A Legend of Brittany.

3. *Josiah Quincy died,* 1864.

We are glad to have the biography of one who, beginning as a gentleman, kept himself such to the end, — who, with no necessity of labor, left behind him an amount of thoroughly done work such as few have accomplished with the mighty help of hunger. Some kind of pace may be got out of the veriest jade by the near prospect of oats ; but the thoroughbred has the spur in his blood.
                              A Great Public Character.

4. *Independence Day ; N. Hawthorne,* 1804.

We, who believe Life's bases rest
Beyond the probe of chemic test,
Still like our fathers, feel Thee near,
Sure that, while lasts the immutable decree,
The land to Human Nature dear
Shall not be unbeloved of Thee.

AN ODE FOR THE FOURTH OF JULY.

New England's poet, soul reserved and deep,
November nature with a name of May.   AGASSIZ.

5. *D. G. Farragut,* 1801.

The power of diffusion without being diffuse
would seem to be the highest merit of narration,
giving it that easy flow which is so delightful.

CHAUCER.

6. *John Huss,* 1373.

All thoughts that mould the age begin
Deep down within the primitive soul,
And from the many slowly upward win
    To one who grasps the whole.

AN INCIDENT IN A RAILROAD CAR.

7. *Sheridan died,* 1816.

Nex' thing to knowin' you 're well off is *nut* to
know when y' ain't.

BIRDOFREDUM SAWIN, ESQ., TO MR. HOSEA BIGLOW.

8. *Fitz-Greene Halleck*, 1790.

God's love and man's are of the selfsame blood,
  And He can see that always at the door
Of foulest hearts the angel-nature yet
Knocks to return and cancel all its debt.

A LEGEND OF BRITTANY.

9. *Henry Hallam*, 1777.

The other day (5th July) I marked 98° in the shade, my high-water mark, higher by one degree than I had ever seen it before. I happened to meet a neighbor ; as we mopped our brows at each other, he told me that he had just cleared 100°, and I went home a beaten man. I had not felt the heat before, save as a beautiful exaggeration of sunshine , but now it oppressed me with the prosaic vulgarity of an oven. MY GARDEN ACQUAINTANCE.

10. *John Calvin*, 1509.

The most winsome and wayward of brooks draws now and then some lover's foot to its intimate reserve, while the spirt of a bursting water-pipe gathers a gaping crowd forthwith. CARLYLE.

11. *John Quincy Adams*, 1767.

There is something delightfully absurd in six volumes addressed to a world of such "vulgar fellows " as Thoreau affirmed his fellow-men to be.

THOREAU.

12. *H. D. Thoreau, 1817.*

He had watched Nature like a detective who is to go upon the stand ; as we read him, it seems as if all-out-of-doors had kept a diary and become its own Montaigne ; we look at the landscape as in a Claude Lorraine glass ; compared with his, all other books of similar aim, even White's " Selborne," seem dry as a country clergyman's meteorological journal in an old almanac. THOREAU.

13. *Ordinance of* 1787 *passed.*

All free governments, whatever their name, are reality governments by public opinion, and it is ne quality of this public opinion that their prosperity depends. It is, therefore, their first duty to purify the element from which they draw the breath of life. DEMOCRACY.

14. *Jane Welsh Carlyle,* 1801.

No man, I suspect, ever lived long in the country without being bitten by these meteorological ambitions. He likes to be hotter and colder, to have been more deeply snowed up, to have more trees and larger blown down than his neighbors. With us descendants of the Puritans especially, these weather-competitions supply the abnegated excitement of the race-course. MY GARDEN ACQUAINTANCE.

15. *Cardinal Manning*, 1808.

The longer on this earth we live
And weigh the various qualities of men,
Seeing how most are fugitive,
Or fitful gifts, at best, of now and then,
Wind-wavered corpse-lights, daughters of the fen,
The more we feel the high stern-featured beauty
Of plain devotedness to duty,
Steadfast and still, nor paid with mortal praise,
But finding amplest recompense
For life's ungarlanded expense
In work done squarely and unwasted days.

UNDER THE OLD ELM.

16. *Sir Joshua Reynolds*, 1723.

They have half-way conquered Fate
Who go half-way to meet her.

A GLANCE BEHIND THE CURTAIN.

17. *Isaac Watts*, 1674.

From the days of the first grandfather, everybody
has remembered a golden age behind them !

CARLYLE.

18. *W. M. Thackeray*, 1811.

The quiet unconcern with which he [Chaucer]
says his best things is peculiar to him among English poets, though Goldsmith, Addison, and Thackeray have approached it in prose.   CHAUCER.

19. *Alexander Dallas Bache*, 1806.

Wonderful, to him that has eyes to see it rightly, is the newspaper. To me, for example, sitting on the critical front bench of the pit, in my study here in Jaalam, the advent of my weekly journal is as that of a strolling theatre, or rather of a puppet-show, on whose stage, narrow as it is, the tragedy, comedy, and farce of life are played in little. Behold the whole huge earth sent to me hebdomadally in a brown paper wrapper !

SERMON OF THE REV. HOMER WILBUR.

20. *John Sterling*, 1806.

For the individual man there is no radical cure, outside of human nature itself, for the evils to which human nature is heir. The rule will always hold good that you must

> Be your own palace or the world's your gaol.

But for artificial evils, for evils that spring from want of thought, thought must find a remedy some-where. DEMOCRACY.

21. *Battle of Bull Run*, 1861.

Our civil war, by the breadth of its proportions and the implacability of its demands, forced us to admit a truer valuation, and gave us, in our own despite, great soldiers and sailors, allowed for such by all the world. A GREAT PUBLIC CHARACTER.

22. *Garibaldi*, 1807.

I am one of those who believe that the real will never find an irremovable basis till it rests on the ideal.   DEMOCRACY.

23. *U. S. Grant died*, 1885.

The one touch of nature that makes the whole world kin is a touch of heroism, our sympathy with which dignifies and ennobles.   GARFIELD.

24. *Simon Bolivar*, 1783.

'T were glorious, no doubt, to be
One of the strong-winged Hierarchy,
To burn with Seraphs, or to shine
With Cherubs, deathlessly divine ;
Yet I, perhaps, poor earthly clod,
Could I forget myself in God,
Could I but find my nature's clew
Simply as birds and blossoms do,
And but for one rapt moment know
'T is Heaven must come, not we must go,
Should win my place as near the throne
As the pearl-angel of its zone,
And God would listen 'mid the throng
For my one breath of perfect song,
That, in its simple human way,
Said all the Host of Heaven could say.
                    WHAT RABBI JEHOSHA SAID.

25. *St. James.*

Once to every man and nation comes the moment to
　　decide,
In the strife of Truth with Falsehood, for the good
　　or evil side ;
Some great cause, God's new Messiah, offering each
　　the bloom or blight,
Parts the goats upon the left hand, and the sheep
　　upon the right.　　　THE PRESENT CRISIS.

26. *Winthrop Mackworth Praed,* 1802.

There is only one thing better than tradition, and
that is the original and eternal life out of which all
tradition takes its rise.　　　THOREAU.

27. *Thomas Campbell,* 1777.

Solitude is as needful to the imagination as society
is wholesome for the character.　　　DRYDEN.

28. *Revolution of July,* 1830.

There is a great deal more than is commonly sup-
posed in this choice of words.　Men's thoughts and
opinions are in a great degree vassals of him who
invents a new phrase or reapplies an old epithet.
The thought or feeling a thousand times repeated
becomes his at last who utters it best.　　　KEATS.

29. *Alexis de Tocqueville*, 1805.

Man is more than Constitutions ; better rot beneath
    the sod,
Than be true to Church and State, while we are
    doubly false to God !

ON THE CAPTURE OF FUGITIVE SLAVES NEAR WASHINGTON.

30. *Samuel Rogers*, 1763.

We have picked nearly every apple (wormy or
otherwise) from the world's tree of knowledge, and
that without an Eve to tempt us. Two or three
have hitherto hung luckily beyond reach on a lofty
bough shadowing the interior of Africa, but there is
a German Doctor at this very moment pelting at
them with sticks and stones.   AT SEA.

31. *John Ericsson*, 1803.

We are comforted by being told that . . . we are
only complying with what is called the Spirit of the
Age, which may be, after all, only a finer name for
the mischievous goblin known to our forefathers as
Puck. I have seen several Spirits of the Age in
my time, of very different voices and summoning in
very different directions, but unanimous in their pro-
pensity to land us in the mire at last.

HARVARD ANNIVERSARY ADDRESS.

1. *Lammas.*

The hope of Truth grows stronger, day by day ;
I hear the soul of Man around me waking,
Like a great sea, its frozen fetters breaking,
And flinging up to heaven its sunlit spray,
Tossing huge continents in scornful play,
And crushing them with din of grinding thunder,
That makes old emptinesses stare in wonder.

Sub Pondere Crescit.

2. *Edward A. Freeman,* 1823.

Poets have sung all manner of vegetable loves ;
Petrarch has celebrated the laurel, Chaucer the
daisy, and Wordsworth the gallows tree.

Carlyle.

3. *Juliana Horatia Ewing,* 1841.

The capacity of indignation makes an essential
part of the outfit of every honest man, but I am in-
clined to doubt whether he is a wise one who allows
himself to act upon its first hints. It should be
rather, I suspect, a *latent* heat in the blood, which
makes itself felt in character.

On a Certain Condescension in Foreigners.

4. *Shelley,* 1792.

Eyes are not so common as people think, or poets
would be plentier.   A Good Word for Winter.

5. *First telegraphic message across the Atlantic,* 1858.

> Letters have sympathies
> And tell-tale faces . . . .
> But now Fate stuns as with a mace ;
> The savage from the skies that men have caught
> And some scant use of language taught,
> Tells only what he must, —
> The steel cold fact in one laconic thrust.
>
> AGASSIZ.

6. *Lord Tennyson,* 1809.

The dainty trick of Tennyson cloys when caught by a whole generation of versifiers, as the *style* of a great poet never can be.   SWINBURNE'S TRAGEDIES.

7. *Joseph Rodman Drake,* 1795.

Truth is quite beyond the reach of satire. There is so brave a simplicity in her, that she can no more be made ridiculous than an oak or a pine.

LETTER OF THE REV. HOMER WILBUR.

8. *Defeat of Spanish Armada,* 1588.

The code of society is stronger with most persons than that of Sinai, and many a man who would not scruple to thrust his fingers in his neighbor's pocket would forego green peas rather than use his knife as a shovel.   POPE.

9. *John Dryden*, 1631.

English blood, made up of the best drops from the veins of many conquering, organizing, and colonizing races, is a blood to be proud of, and most plainly vindicates its claim to dominion when it recognizes kinship through sympathy with what is simple, steadfast, and religious in character. When we learn to respect each other for the good qualities in each, we are helping to produce and foster them.

GARFIELD.

10. *Sir Charles James Napier*, 1782.

Why, law an' order, honor, civil right,
Ef they *ain't* wuth it, wut *is* wuth a fight ?
I'm older 'n you : the plough, the axe, the mill,
All kin's o' labor an' all kin's o' skill,
Would be a rabbit in a wild-cat's claw,
Ef 't warn't for thet slow critter, 'stablished law ;
Onsettle *thet*, an' all the world goes whiz,
A screw 's gut loose in everythin' there is :

MASON AND SLIDELL : A YANKEE IDYLL.

11. *Jeffries Wyman*, 1814.

Let us be of good cheer, however, remembering that the misfortunes hardest to bear are those which never come.

DEMOCRACY.

12. *Robert Southey*, 1774.

There never yet was flower fair in vain,
Let classic poets rhyme it as they will ;
The seasons toil that it may blow again,
And summer's heart doth feel its every ill ;
Nor is a true soul ever born for naught.

SONNET XI.

13. *Battle of Blenheim*, 1704.

I love to l'iter there while night grows still,
An' in the twinklin' villages about,
Fust here, then there, the well-saved lights goes
      out,
An' nary sound but watch-dogs' false alarms,
Or muffled cock-crows from the drowsy farms,
Where some wise rooster (men act jest thet way)
Stands to 't thet moon-rise is the break o' day :
(So Mister Seward sticks a three-months' pin
Where the war 'd oughto eend, then tries agin ;
My gran'ther's rule was safer 'n 't is to crow :
Don't never prophesy — onless ye know.)

MASON AND SLIDELL : A YANKEE IDYLL.

14. *Park Benjamin*, 1809.

I suppose Nature made the donkey half abstract-
edly, while she was feeling her way up to her ideal
in the horse, and that his bray is in like manner an
experimental sketch for the neigh of her finished
animal.

ITALY.

15. *Napoleon Bonaparte*, 1769; *Walter Scott*, 1771.

I can conceive of no healthier reading for a boy, or girl either, than Scott's novels, or Cooper's, to speak only of the dead. I have found them very good reading at least for one young man, for one middle-aged man, and for one who is growing old. No, no — banish the Antiquary, banish Leather Stocking, and banish all the world ! Let us not go about to make life duller than it is.

BOOKS AND LIBRARIES.

The poet's lyre demands
An arm of tougher sinew than the sword.

A GLANCE BEHIND THE CURTAIN.

16. *James Walker*, 1794.

We hear it said sometimes that this is an age of transition, as if that made matters clearer ; but can any one point us to an age that was not ? If he could, he would show us an age of stagnation.

DEMOCRACY.

17. *Fredrika Bremer*, 1801.

'T is heaven alone that is given away,
'T is only God may be had for the asking.

THE VISION OF SIR LAUNFAL.

18. *T. W. Parsons*, 1819.

Use can make sweet the peach's shady side,
That only by reflection tastes of sun.

THE CATHEDRAL.

19. *Béranger*, 1780.

Yet for a moment I was snatched away
And had the evidence of things not seen ;
For one rapt moment ; then it all came back,
This age that blots out life with question-marks,
This nineteenth century with its knife and glass.

THE CATHEDRAL.

20. *Robert Herrick*, 1591.

We have at last got over the superstition that shepherds and shepherdesses are any wiser or simpler than other people.

SPENSER.

Truth, after all, wears a different face to everybody, and it would be too tedious to wait till all were agreed. She is said to lie at the bottom of a well, for the very reason, perhaps, that whoever looks down in search of her sees his own image at the bottom, and is persuaded not only that he has seen the goddess, but that she is far better-looking than he had imagined.

DEMOCRACY.

21. *John Tyndall*, 1820.

True Power was never born of brutish Strength.

PROMETHEUS.

22. *Battle of Bosworth Field*, 1485.

Three-story larnin' 's pop'lar now ; I guess
We thriv' ez wal on jes' two stories less,
For it strikes me ther' 's sech a thing ez sinnin'
By overloadin' children's underpinnin'.

SUNTHIN' IN THE PASTORAL LINE.

23. *Cuvier*, 1769.

We learned once for all that compromise makes a good umbrella but a poor roof. DEMOCRACY.

24. *William Wilberforce*, 1759.

Life is continually weighing us in very sensitive scales, and telling every one of us precisely what his real weight is to the last grain of dust. Whoever at fifty does not rate himself quite as low as most of his acquaintance would be likely to put him, must be either a fool or a great man.

ON A CERTAIN CONDESCENSION IN FOREIGNERS.

25. *Bret Harte*, 1839.

I believe that in all really great imaginative work we are aware, as in nature, of something far more deeply interfused with our consciousness, underlying the obvious and familiar, as the living spirit of them, and accessible only to a heightened sense and a more passionate sympathy. DON QUIXOTE.

26. *Prince Albert*, 1819.

No Godlike thing knows aught of less and less,
But widens to the boundless Perfectness.

SONNET 17.

27. *Titian died*, 1576.

As in the old fairy-tales, the task which the age imposes on its poet is to weave its straw into a golden tissue ; and when every device has failed, in comes the witch Imagination, and with a touch the miracle is achieved, simple as miracles always are after they are wrought. SPENSER.

28. *Goethe*, 1749.

The figure of Goethe is grand, it is rightfully pre-eminent, it has something of the calm, and something of the coldness, of the immortals : but the Valhalla of German letters can show one form, in its simple manhood, statelier even than his.

LESSING.

Goethe taught the self-culture that results in self-possession, in breadth and impartiality of view, and in equipoise of mind ; Wordsworth inculcated that self-development through intercourse with man and nature which leads to self-sufficingness, self-sustainment, and equilibrium of character.

ADDRESS AS PRESIDENT OF THE WORDSWORTH SOCIETY.

29. *O. W. Holmes*, 1809.

Holmes's rockets curve their long ellipse,
And burst in seeds of fire that burst again
To drop in scintillating rain.   AGASSIZ.

30. *Joseph Dennie*, 1768.

There are two kinds of genius. The first and highest may be said to speak out of the eternal to the present, and must compel its age to understand *it*. The second understands its age, and tells it what it wishes to be told. Let us find strength and inspiration in the one, — amusement and instruction in the other, and be honestly thankful for both.   POPE.

31. *John Bunyan died*, 1688.

He's true to God who's true to man ; wherever
  wrong is done,
To the humblest and the weakest, 'neath the all be-
  holding sun,
That wrong is also done to us.
ON THE CAPTURE OF CERTAIN FUGITIVE SLAVES.

SEPTEMBER

1. *Battle of Sedan*, 1870.

Great wars come and great wars go,
Wolf-tracks light on polar snow ;
We shall see him come and gone,
This second-hand Napoleon.
VILLA FRANCA, 1859.

2. *John Howard*, 1726.

For Wisdom is meek sorrow's patient child,
And empire over self, and all the deep
Strong charities that make men seem like gods ;
And love, that makes them be gods, from her
    breasts
Sucks in the milk that makes mankind one blood.

PROMETHEUS.

3. *Oliver Cromwell died*, 1658:

We were designed in the cradle, perhaps earlier,
and it is in finding out this design, and shaping ourselves to it, that our years are spent wisely. It is
the vain endeavor to make ourselves what we are
not that has strewn history with so many broken
purposes and lives left in the rough.   KEATS.

4. *Phœbe Cary*, 1824.

Whatever the ratio of population, the average
amount of human nature to the square mile is the
same the world over.   A MOOSEHEAD JOURNAL.

5. *Richelieu*, 1585.

Time Was unlocks the riddle of Time Is,
That offers choice of glory or of gloom ;
The solver makes Time Shall Be surely his.

THE WASHERS OF THE SHROUD

6. *Lafayette,* 1757.

What was that sigh which seemed so near,
Chilling your fancy to the core ?
'T is only the sad old sea you hear,
That seems to seek forevermore
Something it cannot find, and so,
Sighing, seeks on, and tells its woe
To the pitiless breakers of Appledore.

PICTURES FROM APPLEDORE.

7. *Queen Elizabeth,* 1533.

I know one person who is singular enough to
think Cambridge the very best spot on the habit-
able globe. "Doubtless God *could* have made a
better, but doubtless he never did."

ON A CERTAIN CONDESCENSION IN FOREIGNERS.

8. *Ariosto,* 1474.

I 'm older 'n you, an' I 've seen things an' men,
An' *my* experunce — tell ye wut it 's ben.
Folks thet worked thorough was the ones thet thriv,
But bad work follers ye ez long 's ye live ;
You can't git red on't : jest ez sure ez sin,
It 's ollers askin' to be done agin.

· · · · · · · · ·

Wal, don't give up afore the ship goes down :
It 's a stiff gale, but Providence wun't drown ;

MASON AND SLIDELL : A YANKEE IDYLL.

9. *Battle of Flodden*, 1513.

Every man is conscious that he leads two lives, —
. . . one which he carries to society and the dinner-
table, the other in which his youth and aspiration
survive for him, and which is a confidence between
himself and God. Both may be equally sincere,
and there need be no contradiction between them.

ROUSSEAU AND THE SENTIMENTALISTS.

10. *Mungo Park*, 1771.

God is the only being who has time enough ; but
a prudent man, who knows how to seize occasion,
can commonly make a shift to find as much as he
needs.

ABRAHAM LINCOLN.

11. *James Thomson*, 1700.

New faculties stretch out to meet new wants.

THE PIONEERS.

12. *Charles Dudley Warner*, 1829.

Autumn is the poet of the family. He gets you
up a splendor that you would say was made out of
real sunset ; but it is nothing more than a few
hectic leaves when all is done. He is but a senti-
mentalist after all ; a kind of Lamartine whining
along the ancestral avenues he has made bare tim-
ber of.

A GOOD WORD FOR WINTER.

13. *James Shirley*, 1596.

The only faith that wears well and holds its color in all weathers is that which is woven of conviction.

ABRAHAM LINCOLN.

14. *Humboldt*, 1769.

The Mysterious bounds nothing now on the North, South, East, or West. We have played Jack Horner with our earth, till there is never a plum left in it.

AT SEA.

15. *James Fenimore Cooper*, 1789.

There is one thing in Cooper I like, too, and
    that is
That on manners he lectures his countrymen gratis;
Not precisely so either, because, for a rarity,
He is paid for his tickets in unpopularity.   .
Now he may overcharge his American pictures,
But you 'll grant there 's a good deal of truth in his
    strictures ;
And I honor the man who is willing to sink
Half his present repute for the freedom to think,
And, when he has thought, be his cause strong or
    weak,
Will risk t' other half for the freedom to speak,
Caring naught for what vengeance the mob has in
    store,
Let that mob be the upper ten thousand or lower.

A FABLE FOR CRITICS.

16. *Francis Parkman,* 1823.

Men think it is an awful sight
  To see a soul just set adrift
On that drear voyage from whose night
  The ominous shadows never lift ;
But 't is more awful to behold
  A helpless infant newly born,
Whose little hands unconscious, hold
  The keys of darkness and of morn.

EXTREME UNCTION.

17. *Settlement of Boston,* 1630.

Both by its history and position, the town had what the French call a solidarity, an almost personal consciousness, rare anywhere, rare especially in America.   A GREAT PUBLIC CHARACTER.

18. *Samuel Johnson,* 1709.

Johnson neither in amplitude of literature nor exactness of scholarship could be deemed a match for Lessing ; but they were alike in the power of readily applying whatever they had learned, whether for purposes of illustration or argument. They resemble each other, also, in a kind of absolute common-sense, and in the force with which they could plant a direct blow with the whole weight both of their training and their temperament behind it.   LESSING.

19. *Garfield died*, 1881.

That death-scene was more than singular ; it was unexampled. The whole civilized world was gathered about it in the breathless suspense of anxious solicitude, listened to the difficult breathing, counted the fluttering pulse, was cheered by the momentary rally and saddened by the inevitable relapse. And let us thank God and take courage when we reflect that it was through the manliness, the patience, the religious fortitude of the splendid victim that the tie of human brotherhood was thrilled to a consciousness of its sacred function.

GARFIELD.

20. *Lord Falkland killed*, 1643.

Why make me moan
For loss that doth enrich us yet
With upward yearnings of regret ?

MEMORIÆ POSITUM.

21. *St. Matthew.*

God sends his teachers unto every age,
To every clime, and every race of men,
With revelations fitted to their growth.

RHŒCUS.

22. *Theodore Winthrop*, 1828.

The nurse of full-grown souls is solitude.

COLUMBUS.

23. *Karl Theodore Korner*, 1791.

Science was Faith once ; Faith were Science now,
Would she but lay her bow and arrows by,
And arm her with the weapons of the time.
Nothing that keeps thought out is safe from
      thought ;
For there 's no virgin-fort but self-respect,
And Truth defensive hath lost hold on God.
Shall we treat Him as if He were a child
That knew not His own purpose ? nor dare trust
The Rock of Ages to their chemic tests,
Lest some day the all-sustaining base divine
Should fail from under us, dissolved in gas ?

THE CATHEDRAL.

24. *Sharon Turner*, 1768.

It ever is weak falsehood's destiny
That her thick mask turns crystal to let through
The unsuspicious eyes of honesty.

A LEGEND OF BRITTANY.

25. *Felicia Hemans*, 1794.

How shimmer the low flats and pastures bare,
  As with her nectar Hebe Autumn fills,
  The bowl between me and those distant hills,
And smiles and shakes abroad her misty, tremulous
    hair !   AN INDIAN-SUMMER REVERIE.

SEPTEMBER 26-29

26. *James A. Hillhouse,* 1789.

The foolish and the dead alone never change their opinion. ABRAHAM LINCOLN.

27. *Samuel Adams,* 1722.

Solid success must be based on solid qualities and the honest culture of them. CARLYLE.

28. *Prosper Merimée,* 1803.

Brain is always to be bought, but passion never comes to market. ITALY.

29. *Michaelmas.*

Rabbi Jehosha used to say
That God made angels every day,
Perfect as Michael and the rest
First brooded in creation's nest,
Whose only office was to cry
Hosanna! once, and then to die ;
Or rather, with Life's essence blent,
To be led home from banishment.
Rabbi Jehosha had the skill
To know that Heaven is in God's will ;
And doing that, though, for a space
One heart-beat long, may win a grace
As full of grandeur and of glow
As Princes of the Chariot know.
WHAT RABBI JEHOSHA SAID.

30. *Empress Augusta of Germany,* 1811.

Far through the memory shines a happy day,
Cloudless of care, down-shod to every sense,
And simply perfect from its own resource,
As to a bee the new campanula's
Illuminate seclusion swung in air.
Such days are not the prey of setting suns,
Nor ever blurred with mist of after-thought ;
Like words made magical by poets dead,
Wherein the music of all meaning is
The sense hath garnered or the soul divined,
They mingle with our life's ethereal part,
Sweetening and gathering sweetness evermore,
By beauty's franchise disenthralled of time.

THE CATHEDRAL.

OCTOBER

1. *Rufus Choate,* 1799.

Swords grave no name on the long-memoried rock
But moss shall hide it.   THE VOYAGE TO VINLAND.

2. *W. E. Channing died,* 1842.

No power can die that ever wrought for Truth ;
  Thereby a law of Nature it became,
And lives unwithered in its sinewy youth,
  When he who called it forth is but a name.

ELEGY ON THE DEATH OF DR. CHANNING.

3. *George Bancroft*, 1800.

The rapidity with which the human mind levels itself to the standard around it gives us the most pertinent warning as to the company we keep. It is as hard for most characters to stay at their own average point in all companies as for a thermometer to say 65° for twenty-four hours together.

A MOOSEHEAD JOURNAL.

4. *Guizot*, 1787.

Much did he, and much well ; yet most of all
I prized his skill in leisure and the ease
Of a life flowing full without a plan ;
For most are idly busy ; him I call
Thrice fortunate who knew himself to please,
Learned in those arts that make a gentleman.

BANKSIDE.

5. *Jonathan Edwards*, 1703.

Many a boy has hated, and rightly hated, Homer and Horace the pedagogues and grammarians, who would have loved Homer and Horace the poets, had he been allowed to make their acquaintance.

HARVARD ANNIVERSARY ADDRESS.

6. *Jenny Lind*, 1821.

If we cannot make a silk purse out of a sow's ear, so neither can we hope to succeed with the opposite experiment. But we may spoil the silk for its legitimate uses.

BOOKS AND LIBRARIES.

7. *Edgar A. Poe died*, 1849.

God works for all. Ye cannot hem the hope of
  being free
With parallels of latitude, with mountain-range or
  sea. THE CAPTURE.

8. *John Hay*, 1839.

I do not fear to follow out the truth,
Albeit along the precipice's edge.
  A GLANCE BEHIND THE CURTAIN.

9. *Cervantes*, 1547.

There is a moral in " Don Quixote," and a very
profound one, whether Cervantes consciously put it
there or not, and it is this : that whoever quarrels
with the Nature of Things, wittingly or unwittingly,
is certain to get the worst of it. The great diffi-
culty lies in finding out what the Nature of Things
really and perdurably is, and the great wisdom,
after we have made this discovery, or persuaded
ourselves that we have made it, is in accommodat-
ing our lives and actions to it as best we may or
can. DON QUIXOTE.

10. *Robert Gould Shaw*, 1837.

The man who gives his life for a principle has
done more for his kind than he who discovers a new
metal or names a new gas, for the great motors of
the race are moral, not intellectual. DANTE.

11. *Samuel G. Drake,* 1798.

Friendless, on an unknown sea,
Coping with mad waves and more mutinous spirits,
Battled he with the dreadful ache at heart
Which tempts, with devilish subtleties of doubt,
The hermit of that loneliest solitude,
The silent desert of a great New Thought.

L'ENVOI.

12. *Landing of Columbus,* 1492.

One poor day ! —
Remember whose and not how short it is !
It is God's day, it is Columbus's.
A lavish day !   One day, with life and heart,
Is more than time enough to find a world.

COLUMBUS.

Whatever can be known of earth we know,
  Sneered Europe's wise men, in their snail-shells
    curled ;
No ! said one man in Genoa, and that No
  Out of the dark created this New World.

TO W. L. GARRISON.

13. *Elizabeth Fry died,* 1845.

And they who sowed the light shall reap
The golden sheaves of morning.

AN INTERVIEW WITH MILES STANDISH.

14. *William Penn, 1644.*

Every truth of morals must be redemonstrated in the experience of the individual man before he is capable of utilizing it as a constituent of character or a guide in action. A man does not receive the statements that "two and two make four," and that "the pure in heart shall see God," on the same terms. The one can be proved to him with four grains of corn ; he can never arrive at a belief in the other till he realize it in the intimate persuasion of his whole being. This is typified in the mystery of the incarnation.   DANTE.

15. *Virgil, 70 B. C.*

Then, every morn, the river's banks shine bright
With smooth plate-armor, treacherous and frail,
  By the frost's clinking hammers forged at night,
'Gainst which the lancers of the sun prevail,
  Giving a pretty emblem of the day
  When guiltier arms in light shall melt away,
And states shall move free-limbed, loosed from
  , war's cramping mail.
                    AN INDIAN-SUMMER REVERIE.

16. *Albrecht von Haller, 1708.*

The riches of scholarship, the benignities of literature defy fortune and outlive calamity. They are beyond the reach of thief or moth or rust.
                    BOOKS AND LIBRARIES.

17. *Sir John Bowring*, 1792.

Exact justice is commonly more merciful in the long run than pity, for it tends to foster in men those stronger qualities which make them good citizens.　　　　　　　　　　DANTE.

18. *St. Luke.*

The true historical genius, to our thinking, is that which can see the nobler meaning of events that are near him, as the true poet is he who detects the divine in the casual ; and we somewhat suspect the depth of his insight into the past, who cannot recognize the godlike of to-day under that disguise in which it always visits us.　　CARLYLE.

19. *Sir Thomas Browne*, 1605.

Blessèd the natures shored on every side
With landmarks of hereditary thought !
Thrice happy they that wander not lifelong
Beyond near succor of the household faith.
　　　　　　　　　　THE CATHEDRAL.

20. *Thomas Hughes*, 1823.

Evil springs up, and flowers, and bears no seed,
And feeds the green earth with its swift decay,
Leaving it richer for the growth of truth ;
But Good, once put in action or in thought,
Like a strong oak, doth from its boughs shed down
The ripe germs of a forest.　　PROMETHEUS.

21. *Coleridge*, 1772.

We are here to-day not to consider what Coleridge owed to himself, to his family, or to the world, but what we owe to him. Let us at least not volunteer to draw his frailties from their dread abode.
. . . Whatever may have been his faults and weaknesses, he was the man of all his generation to whom we should most unhesitatingly allow the distinction of genius, that is, of one authentically possessed from time to time by some influence that made him better and greater than himself.

ADDRESS ON UNVEILING THE BUST OF COLERIDGE.

22. *Thomas Arnold died*, 1822.

Even as the roots, shut in the darksome earth,
Share in the tree-top's joyance, and conceive
Of sunshine and wide air and wingèd things
By sympathy of nature, so do I
Have evidence of Thee so far above
Yet in and of me !

THE CATHEDRAL.

23. *Francis Jeffrey*, 1773.

All around me every bush and tree
Says Autumn 's here, and Winter soon will be,
Who snows his soft, white sleep and silence over
all.

AN INDIAN-SUMMER REVERIE.

24. *Sir James Mackintosh*, 1765.

The first lesson in reading well is that which teaches us to distinguish between literature and merely printed matter. The choice lies wholly with ourselves. We have the key put into our hands ; shall we unlock the pantry or the oratory ?

Books and Libraries.

25. *Chaucer died*, 1400.

Who is it needs such flawless shafts as Fate ?
What archer of his arrows is so choice,
Or hits the white so surely ?   They are men,
The chosen of her quiver ; nor for her
Will every reed suffice, or cross-grained stick
At random from life's vulgar fagot plucked :
Such answer household ends ; but she will have
Souls straight and clear, of toughest fibre, sound
Down to the heart of hearts.   The Voyage to Vinland.

26. *Count von Moltke*, 1800.

The man of talents possesses them like so many tools, does his job with them, and there an end ; but the man of genius is possessed by it, and it makes him into a book or a life according to its whim.

Cambridge Thirty Years Ago.

27. *Lord Ashburton*, 1774.

No man can jump off his own shadow,
Nor, for that matter, off his own age.   Spenser.

28. *Erasmus*, 1467.

Fear nothing, and hope all things, as the Right
Alone may do securely ; every hour
The thrones of Ignorance and ancient Night
Lose somewhat of their long-usurpèd power,
And Freedom's lightest word can make them shiver
With a base dread that clings to them forever.

To J. R. GIDDINGS.

29. *John Keats*, 1795.

Yes ! the few words which, like great thunder-
drops,
Thy large heart down to earth shook doubtfully,
Thrilled by the inward lightning of its might,
Serene and pure, like gushing joy of light,
Shall track the eternal chords of Destiny,
After the moon-led pulse of ocean stops.

To THE SPIRIT OF KEATS.

30. *Angelica Kauffman*, 1741.

Hide in thine own soul, and surprise
The password of the unwary elves ;
Seek it, thou canst not bribe their spies ;
Unsought, they whisper it themselves.

THE FOOT-PATH.

31. *Halloween.*

The miracle fades out of history,
But faith and wonder and the primal earth
Are born into the world with every child.

THE CATHEDRAL.

1. *All Saints.*

One feast, of holy days the crest,
   I, though no Churchman, love to keep,
All Saints, — the unknown good that rest
   In God's still memory folded deep ;
The bravely dumb that did their deed,
   And scorned to blot it with a name,
Men of the plain heroic breed,
   That loved Heaven's silence more than fame.
ALL SAINTS.

2. *Marie Antoinette,* 1755.

Felt they no pang of passionate regret
For those unsolid goods that seem so much our
    own ?
These things are dear to every man that lives,
And life prized more for what it lends than gives.
Yea, many a tie, by iteration sweet,
Strove to detain their fatal feet ;
And yet the enduring half they chose,
Whose choice decides a man life's slave or king,
The invisible things of God before the seen and
    known :
Therefore their memory inspiration blows
With echoes gathering on from zone to zone.
ODE READ AT CONCORD.

3. *W. C. Bryant,* 1794.

What an antiseptic is a pure life !
EMERSON THE LECTURER.

4. *Guido*, 1575.

To us the leafless autumn is not bare,
Nor winter's rattling boughs lack lusty green.
Our summer hearts make summer's fulness, where
No leaf, or bud, or blossom may be seen :
For nature's life in love's deep life doth lie.

SONNET XXI.

5. *Washington Allston*, 1779.

Each year to ancient friendships adds a ring,
As to an oak, and precious more and more,
Without deservingness or help of ours,
They grow, and, silent, wider spread, each year,
Their unbought ring of shelter or of shade.

UNDER THE WILLOWS.

5. *Cornelius Conway Felton*, 1807.

Truth only needs to be for once spoke out,
And there 's such music in her, such strange
    rhythm,
As makes men's memories her joyous slaves.

A GLANCE BEHIND THE CURTAIN.

7. *William Croswell*, 1804.

The thing we long for, that we are
    For one transcendent moment,
Before the Present poor and bare
    Can make its sneering comment.   LONGING.

8. *Milton died*, 1674.

Slow are the steps of Freedom, but her feet
　Turn never backward : hers no bloody glare ;
Her light is calm, and innocent, and sweet,
　And where it enters there is no despair.

ODE TO FRANCE.

9. *Boston Fire*, 1872.

Every man feels instinctively that all the beautiful sentiments in the world weigh less than a single lovely action.

ROUSSEAU AND THE SENTIMENTALISTS.

10. *Martin Luther*, 1483.

An imperturbable perception of the *real* relations of things is the Saxon's leading quality, . . . less than anything else will he have the sacramental wafer, — that beautiful emblem of our dependence on Him who giveth the daily bread ; less than anything will he have this smeared with that Barmecide butter of fair words.

This is the lovely and noble side of his character. Indignation at this will make him forget crops and cattle ; and this, after so many centuries, will give him at last a poet in the Monk of Eisleben, who shall cut deep on the memory of mankind that brief creed of conscience, — Here am I. God help me : I cannot otherwise.

CHAUCER.

11. *Martinmas.*

I do not mean to say that every one is fitted by nature or inclination for a definite course of study, or indeed for serious study in any sense. I am quite willing that these should " browse in a library," as Dr. Johnson called it, to their hearts' content. It is, perhaps, the only way in which time may be profitably wasted. Books and Libraries.

12. *Richard Baxter*, 1615.

I have observed that what men prize most is a privilege, even if it be that of chief mourner at a funeral. Democracy.

13. *St. Augustine*, 354.

Yea truly, as the sallowing years
Fall from us faster, like frost-loosened leaves
Pushed by the misty touch of shortening days,
   And that unwakened winter nears,
'T is the void chair our surest guests receives,
'T is lips long cold that give the warmest kiss,
'T is the lost voice comes oftenest to our ears ;
We count our rosary by the beads we miss ;
   To me, at least, it seemeth so,
An exile in the land once found divine,
   While my starved fire burns low,
And homeless winds at the loose casement whine
Shrill ditties of the snow-roofed Apennine.

Agassiz.

14. *L. J. M. Daguerre*, 1787.

New occasions teach new duties; Time makes ancient good uncouth;
They must upward still, and onward, who would
keep abreast of Truth.   THE PRESENT CRISIS.

15. *William Cowper*, 1731.

To me Cowper is still the best of our descriptive
poets of every-day wear. And what unobtrusive
skill he has! How he heightens, for example,
your sense of winter-evening seclusion, by the
twanging horn of the postman on the bridge! That
horn has rung in my ears ever since I first heard it,
during the consulate of the second Adams.
                    A GOOD WORD FOR WINTER.

16. *Charles Eliot Norton*, 1827.

Old friends! The writing of those words has
        borne
My fancy backward to the gracious past,
The generous past, when all was possible,
For all was then untried; the years between
Have taught some sweet, some bitter lessons, none
Wiser than this, — to spend in all things else,
But of old friends to be most miserly.
                    UNDER THE WILLOWS.

17. *George Grote*, 1794.

Mere accuracy is to Truth as a plaster-cast to the
marble statue.   HARVARD ANNIVERSARY ADDRESS.

18. *Asa Gray,* 1810.

There is no wind but soweth seeds
Of a more true and open life.

An Incident in a Railroad Car.

19. *Thorwaldsen,* 1770.

The poet's clearer eye should see, in all
Earth's seeming woe, the seed of Heaven's flowers.

Elegy on the Death of Dr. Channing.

20. *Thomas Chatterton,* 1752.

A public library should also have many and full
shelves of political economy, for the dismal science,
as Carlyle called it, if it prove nothing else, will go
far towards proving that theory is the bird in the
bush, though she sing more sweetly than the night-
ingale, and that the millennium will not hasten its
coming in deference to the most convincing string
of resolutions that were ever unanimously adopted
in public meeting. It likewise induces in us a profound and wholesome distrust of social panaceas.

Books and Libraries.

21. *Bryan Waller Procter,* 1787.

Console yourself, dear man and brother, whatever
you may be sure of, be sure at least of this, that
you are dreadfully like other people.

On a Certain Condescension in Foreigners.

22. *George Eliot*, 1819.

There is no work of genius which has not been the delight of mankind, no word of genius to which the human heart and soul have not, sooner or later, responded. But the man whom the genius takes possession of for its pen, for its trowel, for its pencil, for its chisel, *him* the world treats according to his deserts. ROUSSEAU AND THE SENTIMENTALISTS.

I have been told that Emerson and George Eliot agreed in thinking Rousseau's " Confessions " the most interesting book they had ever read. BOOKS AND LIBRARIES.

23. *Ernest Wadsworth Longfellow*, 1845.

The first element of contemporary popularity is undoubtedly the power of entertaining. If a man have anything to tell, the world cannot be expected to listen to him unless he have perfected himself in the best way of telling it. CARLYLE.

24. *H. T. Buckle*, 1821.

Words, ef you keep 'em, pay their keep,
But gabble 's the short cut to ruin ;
It 's gratis, (gals half-price,) but cheap
At no rate ef it henders doin'.
LATEST VIEWS OF MR. BIGLOW.

25. *Lope de Vega*, 1562.

O Land of Promise ! from what Pisgah's height
  Can I behold thy stretch of peaceful bowers,
The golden harvests flowing out of sight,
  Thy nestled homes and sun-illumined towers ?
  Gazing upon the sunset's high-heaped gold,
Its crags of opal and of chrysolite,
  Its deeps on deeps of glory, that unfold
    Still brightening abysses
    And blazing precipices,
Whence but a scanty leap it seems to heaven
    Sometimes a glimpse is given
Of thy more gorgeous realm, thy more unstinted
    blisses.   To THE FUTURE.

26. *Empress Marie Féodorovna*, 1847.

Whoever can endure unmixed delight, whoever
can tolerate music and painting and poetry all in
one, whoever wishes to be rid of thought and to let
the busy anvils of the brain be silent for a time, let
him read in the " Faery Queen." There is the land
of pure heart's ease, where no ache or sorrow of
spirit can enter.   SPENSER.

27. *Frances Anne Kemble*, 1809.

A great writer does not reveal himself here and
there, but everywhere.   CHAUCER.

28. *William Blake,* 1757.

Let us speak plain : There is more force in names
Than most men dream of ; and a lie may keep
Its throne a whole age longer, if it skulk
Behind the shield of some fair-seeming name.

A GLANCE BEHIND THE CURTAIN.

29. *Sir Philip Sidney,* 1554.

The sunshine seems blown off by the bleak wind,
As pale as formal candles lit by day.

AN INDIAN-SUMMER REVERIE.

30. *St. Andrew.*

On a map of the world you may cover Judea with
your thumb, Athens with a finger-tip, and neither of
them figures in the Prices Current ; but they still
lord it in the thought and action of every civilized
man.

HARVARD ANNIVERSARY ADDRESS.

DECEMBER

1. *Alexandra, Princess of Wales,* 1844.

That lifted blade transformed our jangling clans,
Till then provincial, to Americans,
And made a unity of wildering plans ;
Here was the doom fixed : here is marked the date
When this New World awoke to man's estate,
Burnt its last ship and ceased to look behind.

UNDER THE OLD ELM.

DECEMBER 2-4

2. *First Sunday in Advent.*
Darkness is strong, and so is Sin,
But only God endures forever !

VILLA FRANCA.

3. *Mary Lamb*, 1764.

The preludings of Winter are as beautiful as those of Spring. In a gray December day, when, as the farmers say, it is too cold to snow, his numbed fingers will let fall doubtfully a few star-shaped flakes, the snow-drops and anemones that harbinger his more assured reign. Now, and now only, may be seen, heaped on the horizon's eastern edge, those " blue clouds " from forth which Shakespeare says that Mars "doth pluck the masoned turrets." Sometimes, also, when the sun is low, you will see a single cloud trailing a flurry of snow along the southern hills in a wavering fringe of purple. And when at last the real snow-storm comes, it leaves the earth with a virginal look on it that no other of the seasons can rival, — compared with which, indeed, they seem soiled and vulgar.

A GOOD WORD FOR WINTER.

4. *Carlyle*, 1795.

Though not the safest of guides in politics or practical philosophy, his value as an inspirer and awakener cannot be overestimated.

CARLYLE.

DECEMBER 5-8

5. *Martin Van Buren*, 1782.

As matters stand, too, it is beginning to be doubtful whether Parliament and Congress sit at Westminster and Washington or in the editors' rooms of the leading journals, so thoroughly is everything debated before the authorized and responsible debaters get on their legs.   DEMOCRACY.

6. *Richard H. Barham*, 1788.

Simple as it seems, it was a great discovery that the key of knowledge could turn both ways, that it could open as well as lock, the door of power to the many. The only things a New-Englander was ever locked out of were the jails.

NEW ENGLAND TWO CENTURIES AGO.

7. *Allan Cunningham*, 1784.

We may reckon up pretty exactly a man's advantages and defects as an artist ; these he has in common with others, and they are to be measured by a recognized standard ; but there is something in his *genius* that is incalculable.   DANTE.

8. *Horace*, 65 *B. C.*

Therefore think not the Past is wise alone,
For Yesterday knows nothing of the Best,
And thou shalt love it only as the nest
Whence glory-wingèd things to Heaven have flown.

SONNET 18.

DECEMBER 9-12

9. *John Milton,* 1608.

The grand loneliness of Milton in his latter years, while it makes him the most impressive figure in our literary history, is reflected also in his maturer poems by a sublime independence of human sympathy like that with which mountains fascinate and rebuff us.

MILTON.

10. *W. L. Garrison,* 1805.

In a small chamber, friendless and unseen,
  Toiled o'er his types one poor, unlearned young
    man ;
The place was dark, unfurnitured, and mean ; —
  Yet there the freedom of a race began.

To W. L. GARRISON.

11. *Death of Charles XII.,* 1718.

I am conscious that life has been trying to civilize me for now nearly seventy years with what seem to me very inadequate results. *We* cannot afford to wait, but the Race can.

HARVARD ANNIVERSARY ADDRESS.

12. *Heinrich Heine,* 1797.

Skill, wisdom, and even wit are cumulative ; but that diviner faculty, which is the spiritual eye, though it may be trained and sharpened, cannot be added to by taking thought.

CARLYLE.

13. *Arthur Penrhyn Stanley*, 1815.

We, listening, learned what makes the might of
    words, —
Manhood to back them, constant as a star.

On Board the '76.

I think the one leading characteristic of Dean
Stanley — and I say it to his praise — was the
amount of human nature there was in him.

Stanley.

14. *Washington died*, 1799.

Our sense, refined with virtue of the spot,
    Across the mists of Lethe's sleepy stream
Recalls him, the sole chief without a blot,
    No more a pallid image and a dream
But as he dwelt with men decorously supreme.

Under the Old Elm.

15. *Henry Chorley*, 1808.

He could interpret well the wondrous voices
    Which to the calm and silent spirit come ;
He knew that the One Soul no more rejoices
    In the star's anthem than the insect's hum.
He in his heart was ever meek and humble,
    And yet with kindly pomp his numbers ran,
As he foresaw how all things false should crumble
    Before the free, uplifted soul of man.   Ode.

16. *Boston Tea Party*, 1773.

It is good for us to commemorate this homespun past of ours ; good, in these days of a reckless and swaggering prosperity, to remind ourselves how poor our fathers were, and that we celebrate them because for themselves and their children they chose wisdom and understanding and the things that are of God rather than any other riches.

HARVARD ANNIVERSARY ADDRESS.

17. *Beethoven*, 1770.

One can't bear Strauss when his nature is cloven
To its deeps within deeps by the stroke of Beethoven.   A FABLE FOR CRITICS.

We feel all through it, [Paradise Lost] as in the symphonies of Beethoven, a great controlling reason, in whose safe-conduct we trust implicitly.   MILTON.

18. *Charles Wesley*, 1708.

You may disarm the hands, but not the brains, of a people, and to know what should be defended is the first condition of successful defense.

NEW ENGLAND TWO CENTURIES AGO.

19. *J. M. W. Turner died*, 1851.

Our nipping climate hardly suits
The ripening of ideal fruits.

STUDIES FOR TWO HEADS.

20. *John Wilson Croker*, 1780.

How much more admirable is this tawny vigor, the badge of fruitful toil, than the crop of early muscle that heads out under the forcing glass of the gymnasium !

ITALY.

21. *Leopold von Ranke*, 1795.

There was never colony save this that went forth, not to seek gold, but God.

ON A CERTAIN CONDESCENSION IN FOREIGNERS.

22. *Landing of the Pilgrims*, 1620.

Did they flee from persecution to become themselves persecutors in turn ? This means only that they would not permit their holy enterprise to be hindered or their property to be damaged even by men with the most pious intentions and as sincere, if not always so wise, as they. They would not stand any nonsense, as the phrase is, a mood of mind from which their descendants seem somewhat to have degenerated. They were no more unreasonable than the landlady of Taylor the Platonist in refusing to let him sacrifice a bull to Jupiter in her back-parlor.

HARVARD ANNIVERSARY ADDRESS.

23. *Sainte-Beuve*, 1804.

Within the hall are song and laughter,
  The cheeks of Christmas glow red and jolly ;
And sprouting is every corbel and rafter,
  With lightsome green of ivy and holly.

THE VISION OF SIR LAUNFAL.

24. *Matthew Arnold*, 1822.

A graciousness in giving that doth make
The small'st gift greatest, and a sense most meek
Of worthiness, that doth not fear to take
From others.

IRENE.

25. *Sir Isaac Newton*, 1642.

Walking the New Earth,
Lo, a divine One
Greets all men godlike,
Calls them his kindred,
He, the Divine.

Is it Thor's hammer
Rays in his right hand ?
Weaponless walks he ;
It is the White Christ,
Stronger than Thor.

THE VOYAGE TO VINLAND.

26. *Thomas Gray*, 1716.

Not what we give, but what we share, —
For the gift without the giver is bare.

THE VISION OF SIR LAUNFAL.

27. *St. John Evangelist.*

Yet after he was dead and gone,
  And e'en his memory dim,
Earth seemed more sweet to live upon,
  More full of love, because of him.

THE SHEPHERD OF KING ADMETTUS.

28. *C. M. Sedgwick*, 1789.

For love is blind but with the fleshly eye,
That so its inner sight may be more clear ;
And outward shows of beauty only so
Are needful at the first, as is a hand
To guide and to uphold an infant's steps :
Great spirits need them not, their earnest look
Pierces the body's mask of thin disguise,
And beauty ever is to them revealed,
Behind the unshapeliest, meanest lump of clay,
With arms outstretched and eager face ablaze,
Yearning to be but understood and loved.

LOVE.

29. *W. E. Gladstone*, 1809.

Of one thing, at least, we may be certain, that,
under whatever method of helping things to go
wrong man's wit can contrive, those who have the
divine right to govern will be found to govern in the
end, and that the highest privilege to which the
majority of mankind can aspire is that of being gov-
erned by those wiser than they.

DEMOCRACY.

30. *George H. Lewes died*, 1878.

Whatever of true life there was in thee
    Leaps in our age's veins ;
Wield still the bent and wrinkled empery,
    And shake thine idle chains ; —
  To thee thy dross is clinging,
For us thy martyrs die, thy prophets see,
  Thy poets still are singing.

Here, mid the bleak waves of our strife and care,
    Float the green Fortunate Isles
Where all thy hero-spirits dwell, and share
    Our martyrdoms and toils ;
  The present moves attended
With all of brave and excellent and fair
  That made the old time splendid.

To the Past.

31. *James T. Fields*, 1816.

Cast leaves and feathers rot in last year's nest ;
The wingèd brood, flown thence, new dwellings
        plan ;
The serf of his own Past is not a man ;
To change and change is life, to move and never
        rest ; —
Not what we are, but what we hope is best.

The Pioneer.

www.ingramcontent.com/pod-product-compliance
Lightning Source LLC
Chambersburg PA
CBHW032147010726
47493CB00008BA/2614